In this, the fifth book about the fabulously funny Herbert Yadon, Herbert is really out of this world. In fact, he lands — by accident, of course — on the dog-gonedest planet this side of Mars. He finds the intelligent beings there quite different from those on Earth. They actually regard *him* as an inferior being.

What happens to Herbert—and the planet—after he lands is the basis of this humorous tale.

Herbert's Space Trip

Alfred A. Knopf ⚞ *New York*

HERBERT'S SPACE TRIP

by Hazel Wilson

ILLUSTRATED BY KURT WERTH

L.C. Catalog card number: 65-21563

This is a Borzoi Book, Published by Alfred A. Knopf, Inc.

*This book is dedicated to the many boys who
wrote letters asking me to send Herbert into space*

Contents

Herbert's Space Trip

1

A Barrel of Fun

"It's a long pull, lads,
And a strong pull, boys,
And a song as we go,"
sang Herbert, slightly off key but good and
loud. He was encouraging Pete and Donny to
pull a barrel up the steep side of a junior-size
mountain.

"Stop yowling," cried Pete. "You might use
your breath to catch on to the rope and help,
instead of making a noise like a sick cat."

"Chuck and I have already done more than
our share. We pulled it more than halfway,"
argued Herbert.

"Yeah, mostly on level ground. You planned it that way," muttered Pete.

"As president of the *Up in the Air Club*, I had the right to take my turns where I wanted."

"Why can't Mortimer help?" grumbled Donny. "How come folks talk about working like a dog? I never saw a dog work. Let's hitch the rope to Mortimer's collar and let him pull. Up in Newfoundland, or some place, dogs pull carts. Mortimer at least could pull this blankity-blank barrel."

Herbert's dog, Mortimer, stopped sniffing the ground and growled.

"He says he doesn't want to," said Herbert. "Besides, I don't see why Mortimer should have to be the first working dog in Mapleton."

"I'm thinking of resigning from the club right now," threatened Pete.

"You can't resign from the *Up in the Air Club* orally. You have to send in a written resignation," Herbert informed Pete.

"Who says so? It's not in our bylaws."

"Well, it will be the next time I revise the bylaws," declared Herbert. Then, seeing that Pete and Donny really looked winded, he and Chuck took their places. Even Herbert was

4

breathing hard before they reached the top of the hill. All four boys were glad to sit on a flat rock and rest.

Herbert and his three best friends — Pete, the mayor's son, Donny, who had the biggest ears of any boy in town, and Chuck, whose father was a house painter — were about to conduct an experiment. As part of their training to be future astronauts, they were going to test their reactions to speed and motion by rolling down a steep hill in a barrel. The fact that the nearest very steep hill was three miles from Mapleton had made hauling the barrel that far somewhat of a chore.

"One good thing about climbing a hill," thought Herbert, "is that you get to see what's on the other side." He looked down the hillside and saw, close to its foot, a tall, towerlike structure attached to a long, one-story building more like a shed than a house.

"That tower is shaped like a silo, but it doesn't exactly look like a silo," thought Herbert.

"My father says that the old geezer living down there is a hermit," said Pete.

"I thought a hermit was a cookie with raisins in it," remarked Donny.

"One kind of hermit is a cookie, but another kind is a man who lives alone and doesn't want company," explained Herbert.

"My mother makes the best hermits — the cookie kind," said Chuck. "Wish I'd brought along a dozen or so."

"Guess he's only half-hermit, since his wife is with him," said Pete. "My father says the old man bought the property to go in for dairy farming. That's why he built the silo."

"Then where are his cows?" asked Herbert. "A man doesn't build a silo to hold fodder for his cows before he has any cows."

"I suppose *you* know more about it than my father," said Pete with sarcasm.

"Could be," mused Herbert. "After we get through this test, maybe I'll investigate. I still doubt if that tower down there is a silo."

"He won't let you investigate. Pa says he has *No Trespassing* signs all over the place. We'd better make our barrel roll down the side we came up."

"No, we'll go down this side," Herbert decided. "We'll aim the barrel to the left of that tower. Give us a chance to see it close."

"And run the risk of having the old man

come out and pepper us with bird shot?" objected Pete.

"Don't cry before you're hurt," said Herbert cheerfully. "Tell you what, Pete. I'll make it up to you for taking the first turn pulling the barrel. I'll let you have the first turn rolling down in it."

Pete looked down the steep slope with its scattered trees and outcropping of boulders. "I don't want to be selfish about having the first turn. You can go first, Chuck."

"I'd just as soon go last," said Chuck. "You go first, Donny."

"This barrel business was your idea. It's up to you to go first, Herbert. Unless you're scared to," taunted Donny.

"Me scared? Of course I'm not scared. Come to think of it, though, it might be a good idea to let Mortimer make the trial run. It's customary to send animals into space before men try it." Herbert reached down and patted Mortimer. "Good old Mortimer," he said, although Mortimer was not really old. "You're going to be made an honorary member of the *Up in the Air Club* as soon as you make this trial run."

"He comes to all the meetings now," grumbled Pete, but he was all in favor of letting Mortimer make the trial run. So were the other boys.

Mortimer, sensing that something unpleasant was about to happen to him, would not go near the barrel. Herbert had to drag him. Mortimer liked the boys too much to bite, but he barked and yelped all the time the boys were stuffing him in the barrel. Then Herbert had to hold him in.

"All set?" Pete was ready to give the barrel a good push.

Herbert could have stood Mortimer's mournful yelps, but his dog's pleading eyes were too much for him to take. He let go of Mortimer and the dog was out of the barrel like lightning, all but knocking Herbert down in the exuberance of his relief.

"Mortimer might get dizzy and throw up," Herbert said as an excuse. He looked down the steep slope and squared his shoulders. "I always was willing to go first, but I wanted to be big-hearted and let you other guys have turns before me," he said. "I'll go!"

Herbert got in the barrel and scrunched

down until all of him was in. "Let her roll," he ordered bravely.

Three pairs of hands belonging to Herbert's three best friends gave the barrel a vigorous push.

"This is really excellent training for a boy like me who intends to be an astronaut," thought Herbert as the barrel gathered speed and bumped over rocks and roots. "Wish we had made the newspaper padding thicker," he said to himself as an especially hard bump jarred his teeth. "If this doesn't make me dizzy, nothing ever will. Maybe I'll be one of the first passengers to the moon. I'll write to my Uncle Horace and ask him to buy me a round-trip ticket to the moon the first time they go on sale. I wish —"

That was all Herbert wished just then. The barrel, rolling with terrific speed, reached the foot of the hill. Its aim had changed after hitting several boulders on the way down. Instead of landing to the left of the tower, it crashed into the long shed attached to it.

Herbert lost consciousness for only a few seconds, but he was too groggy to move. He was barely aware of being lifted out of the barrel and taken into the long shed and put down on a bed.

It felt good to be lying down. He was dizzy and his head ached.

"I'll get some ice and put it on the bump on his forehead," he heard a woman say.

Herbert opened his eyes and saw an old man and an old woman bending over him. The old woman's eyes, in her wrinkled face, were worried and kind. The old man, however, looked more angry than worried. His eyes were as sharp and fierce as an eagle's.

"You and your barrel vehicle are trespassers on private property," the old man scolded in a slightly foreign-sounding accent. "You might have knocked the front of my house down. You might have killed yourself. Do you know that?"

"Oh, I don't kill that easy," said Herbert, sitting up and feeling better already. Then, while holding a cloth with ice in it to his forehead, he explained about the *Up in the Air Club* and how rolling down a steep hill in a barrel was preparation for training as an astronaut.

As Herbert talked, the old man's stern expression softened. "So, you have an interest in space travel," he said.

"I sure have." By now, Herbert's eyes were busy examining the long room he was in. Be-

sides being living quarters, the room obviously was some sort of laboratory. Herbert saw a long table cluttered with papers and wall shelves holding bottles, jars, and metal objects. Then Herbert's eyes fairly popped in astonishment at what they beheld at the far end of the room. A big cage held an animal about Herbert's size — a large chimpanzee happily swinging on a bar.

"You keep a chimp. Oh boy, a real chimp!" cried Herbert. "Can I go over and get acquainted with him? I've always wanted to get to know a chimp better. He's big for a chimp, isn't he?"

"He is not a he, he is a she," said the old man.

"Her name is Susy," said the old woman in her gentle voice.

Herbert got up from the bed and would have run to the cage if the old man had not grasped him with a strong hand.

"I do not want it known that I have a chimpanzee on my premises," said the old man sternly. "I demand that you keep the presence of Susy a secret."

"Okay," promised Herbert. "Cross my heart and hope to die if I tell a soul. Though I don't see why you want to keep her a secret. Most anybody would be proud of keeping a pet chimpanzee."

"Pride has nothing to do with it. Nothing. I can trust you? Yes?"

"Double yes," said Herbert, looking the old man squarely in the eye.

"Then, since you are within my house, though without invitation, you understand, you may make a brief acquaintance with Susy." The old man's voice was still stern, yet Herbert had the impression that he was less hard-boiled than he seemed.

Still a bit shaky on his feet, Herbert hurried over to the big cage. On the way, he stole a quick look at the long table cluttered with charts, maps, and pages of figures. "This man is no dairy farmer," thought Herbert, and he was surer than ever that the tower outside was no silo.

"Susy likes to have her head scratched," said the old woman, who had followed Herbert to the cage.

Herbert scratched Susy's head, and she surprised him by reaching out a hairy arm and scratching his.

"Ouch! You're hitting a sore spot," cried

Herbert, pushing the chimp's arm away. Then, afraid he had hurt Susy's feelings, Herbert said soothingly, "If I had known I was coming to see you, I would have brought a banana."

"Susy is very fond of bananas," said the old woman. "That is why my husband has made banana pellets so Susy —" The old woman did not finish her sentence. She looked as though she wished she had not begun it.

"Why banana pellets?" thought Herbert.

"My husband is very careful about Susy's diet," said the old woman, as if that were responsible for her remark about the banana pellets.

"If your husband is an animal doctor, I know a sick dog I'd like to bring to see him," said Herbert, remembering a neighbor's dog whose bark had become unusually hoarse.

"Animal doctor!" The old woman's voice suddenly grew shrill. "My husband is Dr. Johann Gebhart. A pioneer in rocketry, they called him in all Germany. But, when he refused to work for the Nazi regime, we were forced to escape the land in the night. We were refugees, wanderers with no home, until we came to the United States."

"Do not tell more, Elsa," broke in Dr. Gebhart. "My wife has nerves," he said to Herbert. "You will forget, please, anything she has said. You will keep silence about all you have seen or heard here."

Herbert was dying to ask if the tower outside was what he was now suspecting it might be, but he thought it better not to risk arousing the old man's anger.

"I keep my word. I promised and I'll not forget," said Herbert.

A loud barking and knocking at the door announced the fact that Herbert's friends and his dog were outside.

"Took them long enough to get here," thought Herbert. Yet, he was glad they had not come sooner, for his brief stay in Dr. Gebhart's home had proved to be most interesting.

"Must be the other members of the *Up in the Air Club* coming after me," said Herbert.

Dr. Gebhart seized Herbert by the arm and hurried him to the door. "Get them away from here," he ordered. "You will remember your promise. You will not discuss me. You will not tell about Susy."

By now, Dr. Gebhart and Herbert were at the door. Quickly, the old man opened the door, pushed Herbert out, and slammed the door behind him.

The boys and Mortimer greeted Herbert with pleasure and relief.

"You all right?" asked Pete, real concern in his face.

"We sure thought you were a goner when we saw you crash into the hermit's shed," said Donny. "Then, when we saw you being lugged inside, we were afraid you might be dead."

"We kept arguing about which of us would have to tell your mother," said Chuck. "We would have gotten here sooner, only it takes more time to walk down a hill than to roll down. We tried running, but Pete fell down and Donny turned his ankle, and I thought we'd better keep together."

"What happened to the barrel?" asked Herbert.

"Smashed to smithereens," said Pete.

"Good! Then we won't have to drag it home," said Herbert.

The boys climbed back up the junior-size

mountain slowly. They did not talk much. They were going down the other side before Pete thought to ask what it had been like in the old man's shed.

Herbert wished he could share what he had seen with his fellow members of the *Up in the Air Club*, but he remembered his promise. "There was just furniture and stuff there, and the hermit's wife put ice on the bump on my head," he said, keeping a close hold on his tongue.

The boys examined Herbert's bump and each said that he had once had one much worse.

"Did they give you anything to eat?" asked Pete.

"Not even a banana," said Herbert.

"What made you think they might have given you a banana?" asked Chuck.

"I often think about being given a banana. I like bananas," said Herbert. "Wish I had one this minute."

The conversation veered to a discussion of banana ice cream. Pete and Donny didn't like it but Chuck did. He wished he had a dish of two scoops, with half a dozen of his mother's hermits.

For once, Herbert did not contribute much to the conversation. He was too busy thinking. Maybe the silo-looking tower might house a rocket. If Dr. Gebhart really was a pioneer in rocketry, he might have built a rocket — or might be going to build one.

"I've got to find out for sure," thought Herbert. "I'll have to think up some excuse for going back. Soon, too."

2

Inside Information

There was no meeting of the *Up in the Air Club* the following Saturday, the first weekly meeting skipped since the club had been formed two months before. But the president of the club would have been the only member able to attend. On Friday, Pete, Donny, and Chuck all came down with the chicken pox. Herbert thought his friends showed poor timing since it was the last day of school before summer vacation. If Herbert had a disease, he preferred getting it while school was in session.

Herbert had already had the chicken pox, so it was safe for him to visit his friends. He called on Pete, Donny, and Chuck on Saturday morning, but they were too ill to have company.

When Herbert got home, he found his mother making cookies.

"What kind of cookies are you making?" he asked.

"Hermits," said his mother, dropping blobs of dough on a cookie sheet.

Herbert's eyes brightened with a sudden idea. This would be a good time to go to see the Gebharts. "Is it all right for me to take some cookies to my friends this afternoon?" he asked.

"I doubt if Pete, Donny, and Chuck are well enough to eat cookies. Better take them some in a few days, not today."

"Oh, I don't want them for the chicken poxers. They are for friends I met last Saturday. I know they will love your hermits." And he added to himself, "Seems appropriate taking hermits to a hermit." Even though Dr. Gebhart was only half-hermit, since he had his wife with him, Herbert thought he seemed like a hermit — his not liking company and all that.

Herbert's mother seldom refused him anything, unless it were something which would be injurious to him. "Of course you may take some hermits to your new friends. It is good for you to make new friends," she said approvingly. "Where do these new friends of yours live?"

"Oh, out of town a ways." Herbert did not want to be too specific. "Don't I smell something burning?"

Mrs. Yadon rushed to the oven to check the pan of cookies, which saved Herbert from further questioning.

After lunch, Herbert filled a medium-sized paper bag with hermits. His mother said he might take his friends a dozen and a half cookies, and Herbert put in twenty-two for good measure. "If I get hungry on the way and eat four, I'll still have a dozen and a half left," he reasoned.

Herbert remembered to take two bananas for Susy. And he picked a bunch of petunias for Mrs. Gebhart. Then, he was off on his bike, with Mortimer sitting in a crude contraption Herbert had made for him behind the bicycle seat. It was a tight fit for Mortimer so, most of the way, he preferred to run along beside the bicycle. Usually, Mortimer liked to ride better than to run, but not if it meant riding in the contraption at the back of Herbert's bike.

Herbert found it quicker and less tiring riding his bike the three miles than it had been going on foot, dragging a barrel part of the way.

He did not expect to be welcomed with any enthusiasm by the Gebharts, but he hoped they would ask him to come in. He decided that, if they did, he would come right out and ask Dr. Gebhart if that was a silo adjoining the house, or something else. Something like a hangar for a rocket, Herbert thought, his curiosity mounting as he neared the hill. He found the hill too steep to ride up on his bike and too dangerous to ride down on the other side. After all, he did not want to arrive at the Gebhart's door wounded for the second time in a row.

Herbert almost wished he had left his bike at home after he had pushed it up the very steep hill and kept it from getting away from him down the other side. Just before he knocked at the Gebhart's door, he thought, "If they won't let me in, I'll just have to do some snooping," for he was determined to find out what, if anything, was in that tower.

Herbert began to talk the instant the door was opened. He was glad that it was Mrs. Gebhart, not her husband, who came to the door.

"I brought you these to repay you for your kindness to me last week," said Herbert, offering his bunch of petunias. "And here are some hermits for the old — I mean for Dr. Gebhart. My mother makes very good hermits. I'm sorry I squashed one of the bananas I brought for Susy. Will you let me feed them to her? I've always wanted to feed bananas to a chimp."

"Petunias are my favorite flower," said Mrs. Gebhart, smelling the bouquet. "It was thoughtful of you to come way out here to thank us." She hesitated and then smiled at Herbert. "You already know Susy is here and have seen her. I can't see what harm it could do to let you feed her your bananas."

"Send the boy away," shouted Dr. Gebhart, thumping to the door with his cane. It was a strong-looking cane, but Herbert did not back away, even when the old man raised it in a threatening gesture.

"My uncle, Senator Horace B. Frothingham, took me to the St. Louis zoo last summer," said Herbert, speaking very quickly. "I wanted to feed the chimps some bananas, only I didn't happen to have any with me. Here are some hermits for you, sir. I thought you might like them, you being a sort of — I mean I hope you like cookies," he said, being tactful about not calling Dr. Gebhart a hermit to his face.

To Herbert's pleased surprise, Dr. Gebhart's manner entirely changed. He swung the door wide open. "Come right in," he urged. "So, you're Senator Frothingham's favorite nephew. I've heard him speak of you."

"I guess you might say I'm his favorite nephew. Anyway, I'm his only one." Herbert needed no second invitation to come in and Mortimer followed, but not with enthusiasm, since he did not like the smell of the chimpanzee.

While Herbert fed Susy a banana, Dr. Gebhart explained how he happened to know Uncle Horace. It seemed that, in World War II, after refusing to work on rockets for the Nazis, Dr. Gebhart spent several months in a concentration camp. He had escaped but had fallen into the hands of the Russians, who had shipped him to Russia to work in a laboratory.

"I was not ill-treated, but I did not desire to advance the aeronautic experiments of the Russians," he told Herbert. "My wife, meanwhile, had reached Poland, and I was in communication with her. But it was a very long time before I was able to get away. Finally, my wife and I were reunited. But my health was broken, and we had no money and no passports. It was your uncle who visited the refugee camp where we were existing so long without hope and managed, after some delay, to get us to the United States."

"Good for Uncle Horace! He always knows what to do about everything. Or nearly everything," said Herbert, watching Susy peel the second banana. She was a smart chimp and Herbert wished he owned her. Maybe Dr. Gebhart would sell her to him, but this did not appear to be the right time to ask.

"It was your uncle who used his influence to have me employed by the McDougal Aircraft Company. I was of some use to them, but already sixty-eight years old. And their retirement age is seventy. Besides, my reputation in Germany was not too well-known to the younger men of the company. I was not given a free hand, and I work best independently. So, at seventy, I was retired. That was five years ago. Since then,

I have continued my experiments by myself. Only your uncle has encouraged me, both with his belief in my abilities and with money. Soon I hope to show him and the world that I have made much progress in the problems of space travel." The old man's eyes suddenly looked younger than his deeply-lined face.

Herbert had listened with interest to the old man's story. With the mention of space travel, Herbert's eyes shone.

"Not even baseball interests me more than space travel," he said. "Is that what you're working on here? How did you happen to settle near Mapleton? Say, wouldn't it be super if you invent something which will make the place famous? A good many people never have heard of the town, you know, though I hope to do something about that when I grow up, if not sooner."

"Your uncle knew of this vacant property near your home," said Dr. Gebhart. "I had come to the stage in my experiments where I must have space and privacy. And I still choose to have my work remain secret until the success or failure of my latest experiment."

"Couldn't you let just me in on it," begged Herbert. "I wouldn't tell even my parents."

Dr. Gebhart shook his head and Herbert looked very disappointed.

"He is the Senator's favorite nephew and we owe a great deal to the Senator," Mrs. Gebhart reminded her husband.

"Uncle Horace tells me I'm good at keeping a secret, even when it might be better to tell it," said Herbert.

"A secret shared is no longer a secret," said Dr. Gebhart. Then his fierce eyes relented. "At your age, I, too, had a most active curiosity. It is a trait common to all scientists and inventors. Persistence you doubtless possess also. If I do not tell you what is in my tower, what will you do?"

Herbert flushed. "Snoop around and see if I can find out by myself," he confessed.

"At your age, I would have done the same," said Dr. Gebhart with the hint of a smile. "Come, I will show you."

The old man hobbled to the door which opened into the tower, with Herbert so close to his heels that he almost bumped into him. Dr. Gebhart unlocked the door. He snapped on a light inside the tower.

"What a beauty! What a —" Words, for once,

failed Herbert. What he saw inside the building shaped like a silo was a silver cylinder reaching far above his head.

"It's the biggest, most beautiful model rocket I've ever seen. The *Up in the Air Club* expects to build a model rocket this summer, but it will be nothing to compare with this. When are you testing it? Can I come and see it blast off? Please."

"Model rocket!" sputtered Dr. Gebhart. "Do you think I still play with toys? I'll show you that this is no mere model rocket but a real spaceship."

Dr. Gebhart led the way to a ladder at the far side of the rocket. Then, in spite of his lameness, he started up the ladder, as spry as a young man. Up, up he went, with Herbert only a rung behind.

Before Herbert was halfway up the ladder, he saw that there was a door in the side of the rocket. Quivering with excitement, Herbert watched Dr. Gebhart open an outer door and enter an inner space from which he could see another door.

"This rocket has an air lock," thought Herbert, and by now he was convinced that it *was* a

real, not a model, rocket. Yet, even after he had followed Dr. Gebhart into the cockpit, which was large enough for both of them at the same time, there was much Herbert did not understand.

"I know it's a real rocket and not a model one," said Herbert, "but to get into space, I thought a rocket would have to be much bigger than this. I've read lots about rockets and have seen movies and pictures about them. I thought it took a three-stage rocket to get into space."

"Suppose I informed you that I have invented a propellent so highly concentrated that it has sufficient thrust to send an entire rocket into space? That I can send a one-stage rocket into space."

"Gosh!" was all Herbert could think of to say, just then. But Herbert was never long at a loss for words.

"Can I try the driver's — I mean the pilot's seat for size?" he begged.

"If you like. I made it the right size for Susy, and you and she are about the same bigness."

"You mean you are going to send the chimp into space?"

"That is my intention. The automatic pilot

will be set to take Susy to her destination and to return her, after a short interval, to earth."

"You're not sending Susy to the moon?"

"No."

"Then where? To Mars?"

"In the direction of Mars," said Dr. Gebhart.

"Jeepers!" said Herbert.

Herbert sat down in the contour seat where Susy was to half-recline during her flight. It was a pretty good fit for Herbert. He gazed with wonder and interest at the many buttons and levers on the instrument panel, which was even more brilliantly lighted than the rest of the cockpit.

"Light for the cockpit is furnished by a laser," explained Dr. Gebhart. "A laser, in case you are uninformed about such matters, is a light ray. A tiny speck of metal or ruby can convert ten times as much current into light as an ordinary light bulb. Takes the place of more bulky transistors."

"Isn't science wonderful?" marveled Herbert.

"It is indeed," said Dr. Gebhart. Then he went on to explain what the various buttons and levers on the instrument panel were for, rattling off their uses in such technical language that

Herbert only understood about half.

"What's this lever for?" asked Herbert, touching a lever at the far left of the instrument panel.

Dr. Gebhart chuckled. "Susy has been taught to press that lever. It releases a banana pellet up here. They will keep her contented during her long flight."

"And this lever at the far right?"

"I've answered enough questions," said Dr. Gebhart in a way that shut off further questioning from Herbert — for the time being.

Back in his living quarters, Dr. Gebhart seemed almost sociable. He munched hermits, which he declared were very good. And he did not object when Mrs. Gebhart asked if it would be all right if she showed Herbert what was in the closet beside the door which led into the tower.

"Since I have shown him my major invention, I have no objection to having him see a minor one," said Dr. Gebhart.

Mrs. Gebhart opened a closet door and brought out Susy's space suit. Her husband said that it was much lighter in weight than ordinary space suits. Herbert hefted it and was surprised to find how light it was. He was pleased

that Dr. Gebhart did not object to his trying on the bubble-shaped helmet.

"It's just super," Herbert told Dr. Gebhart. "Has Susy tried on her space suit, yet?"

"Naturally. Susy is also accustomed to the cockpit of the rocket. I always wait to put on her space suit until she is in the cockpit and has helped herself to a few banana pellets."

"You've thought of everything," said Herbert with admiration.

"I sincerely hope so," said Dr. Gebhart.

Herbert could sense that Dr. Gebhart thought his visit had lasted long enough. Herbert always did try to leave a place before actually being kicked out. But, before leaving the Gebharts, he went over to the cage for a farewell look at Susy.

"I never thought a time would come when I would envy a chimp," Herbert said, more to himself than to Susy. "You're going way, way out into space and I'd give my bottom dollar — and my top one, too — to be going with you."

Herbert then turned to Dr. Gebhart to ask if he had yet set the date of Susy's flight into space.

"According to the weather forecast, this coming Monday will be fair," said Dr. Gebhart. "That will be the day."

"I'd give anything to be here to see the blast-off," entreated Herbert. "Then I could write Uncle Horace all about it and save you the bother, if you don't like to write letters."

"I had written your uncle to come, but he was unable to get away," said Dr. Gebhart. "Hmmm. Perhaps it is fitting that Senator Frothingham's nephew be present to witness the start of a flight which may revolutionize the construction of aircraft. If you can be here soon after sunrise, you may see Susy take off in the direction of Mars."

"I'd even stay up all night, if need be, to see Susy take off into space," said Herbert, beaming. "I'll be here at the crack of dawn. What a super-duper way to begin my summer vacation!"

3

Going Up

Herbert did not have an alarm clock of his own and he was afraid his mother might ask questions if he borrowed hers. She would be sure to want to know why he was getting up so early on the first Monday of summer vacation. It would be more like him to sleep till ten. Besides, Mrs. Yadon needed the alarm clock to get Mr. Yadon up in time to get to work. So, Herbert had to trust his mental alarm clock. He thought hard before he went to sleep Sunday night that he had to wake up the next morning before dawn. And he did. He was awake by four A.M.

Last night's weather report on TV had said

that the day would be fair but the early morning cool for June, so Herbert dressed in blue jeans and a short-sleeved sport shirt and took his gray sweater. Shoes in hand, he went downstairs, being careful to step over the stair that creaked. Mortimer, who slept in the kitchen when he could not sneak upstairs to sleep with Herbert, would have barked a joyful good morning if Herbert had not grasped him firmly by the muzzle.

"Don't bark," Herbert ordered. "Yes, you may come with me," he answered the pleading look in Mortimer's eyes. "I promised Dr. Gebhart I wouldn't tell anybody about Susy's test flight, but I'm sure he meant people, not dogs."

Not daring to take time for a proper breakfast, Herbert raided the refrigerator for leftover meat loaf, bread and butter, and a couple of apples. He shared the meat loaf with Mortimer. After hastily drinking a pint of cold milk, Herbert was ready to start. He did not forget to take along a banana for Susy. It seemed like a small going-away present, but Herbert did not know anything else that Susy liked.

Herbert pedaled hard and fast out to the steep hill on the outskirts of Mapleton. Morti-

mer had refused to sit for even part of the way
in the contraption behind the bicycle seat, and
had to run hard to keep up. Even Herbert was
out of breath by the time he had gotten his bicycle up and then down the steep hill. By now,
there were bright bands of color in the east, and
it was light enough for Herbert to see that the
aluminum top of the tower had been swung to
one side.

"Don't let it already have happened," Herbert kept saying to himself as he left his bicycle in a hurry and rushed to the shed door.

Mrs. Gebhart answered his impatient knock.
"Oh, it's you," she said, as if she had forgotten
that Herbert was expected. Her wispy hair
looked as if she had not combed it, and there
were extra worry lines in her wrinkled face.

"Send the boy away," roared Dr. Gebhart's
cross voice, but Herbert was already inside.

"You'll find things in a sad state here," said
Mrs. Gebhart.

Herbert saw that Dr. Gebhart was sitting in
a chair with two pails of water on the floor in
front of him. He groaned as he lifted his foot
from one pail and plunged it into the other, the
one which steamed.

"Alternate hot and cold water are good for a sprained ankle," explained Mrs. Gebhart.

"I'm so sorry," said Herbert. "I once sprained my ankle while jumping a very high jump, and I know how it hurts. Here. Let me pour in some more hot water." Herbert picked up the steaming teakettle from the floor beside the pails and poured in a generous amount of nearly boiling water.

Dr. Gebhart pulled out his foot in a hurry. "Are you trying to boil my foot?" he grumbled.

"I was just trying to help."

"This morning I am beyond help," said Dr. Gebhart, and Herbert had never in his life heard anybody sound more discouraged.

"When did you sprain your ankle, sir?" Herbert dared ask.

"On my last trip down the ladder, after taking up all the equipment for Susy's flight. But that's not the worst of it. I would have had my ankle tightly bandaged and, hurt or no hurt, I would have taken Susy up to the cockpit and put on her space suit, but —" Dr. Gebhart stopped to groan.

"Susy is sick," Mrs. Gebhart said sadly. "Poor Susy! I let her sleep until Dr. Gebhart was taking her space suit up the ladder. Then, when I brought her breakfast, I discovered that she was quite feverish. Susy has a very bad cold. It would not be safe to send a chimpanzee into space with a bad cold."

"What a shame! What a rotten shame!" cried Herbert.

Herbert went over to look at Susy and saw that she did not look at all well. She even refused the banana Herbert held out to her.

Dr. Gebhart shifted his foot from the pail of hot water to the pail of cold and let out another groan. "All this soaking is doing it no good," he scolded. "Go get something to bandage it," he ordered his wife. "I have to get that valuable equipment down from the rocket." He pulled his foot from the water and tried to stand. Herbert saw beads of sweat on the old man's forehead, saw him sink back to his chair.

"It's sprained worse than I thought," Dr. Gebhart said, pain and frustration in his eyes.

"I'll go up and bring down all the equipment for you," offered Herbert. "Be glad to. And, after I get that done, I'll go home and bring back some cough medicine for Susy's cold. It tastes awful but it's good for a cold, and I'll be glad to get it used up. It's left over from my last cold."

"You can't bear your weight on that ankle, anyway," Mrs. Gebhart told her husband. "And I'm too unsteady on my feet to climb a ladder. It's providential that Senator Frothingham's favorite nephew is here to help us."

"I hate to trust it to anybody but myself, but I see I'll have to," said Dr. Gebhart. "It will take you three trips, and I think I'll thrash you with my cane if you damage anything," he told Herbert. "For it would take months, if not longer, to replace some of that equipment."

"I'll be very careful," promised Herbert.

"After you get everything down, I'll tell you how to close the top of the tower," said Dr. Gebhart. "It might rain, and I don't want the rocket to get wet."

"Would rain hurt it?" asked Herbert.

"Of course not, but I prefer to keep it dry."

Herbert remembered he had felt that way about his bicycle when it had been new, and he understood how Dr. Gebhart felt about his rocket.

Mortimer wanted to go with Herbert up the ladder to the rocket's cockpit, but Herbert refused to let him try the climb. Mortimer was not good at climbing ladders and Herbert had no intention of carrying him.

"I'll have my arms full coming down and couldn't help you," he explained to Mortimer, who had a hurt look in his eyes. "Don't worry. I'll be right back."

Once up the ladder and in the cockpit, however, Herbert was in no hurry to leave. He figured that this might be his last chance, before he was grown up, to be inside the cockpit of a real rocket. Nor did he resist the impulse to try on Susy's space suit, not wanting to wait until he was an astronaut to have one on. Susy's space suit fitted Herbert nicely, although the sleeves were a bit too long.

Seeing the valve where a small hose was to be attached for putting pressure in the space suit, Herbert made the connection. He then attached the oxygen tank, feeling proud of himself for knowing what each piece of equipment was for. With all this apparatus on, Herbert sat down in Susy's reclining chair. Having gone this far, it seemed the thing to do to adjust and fasten the straps which were to hold the chimpanzee in place. Herbert now faced the instrument panel with its many buttons and levers.

"Wish Dr. Gebhart would let me go in Susy's place," Herbert thought, but he knew that the old man would never consent to that. So, Herbert sat for a few minutes, pretending he was making a flight through space. He even pressed the lever to the far left which released a banana pellet. It came out like bubble gum from a gum-dispensing machine. The taste was like a blend of cough drop and banana, and Herbert did not care much for it.

Herbert remembered the functions of most of the buttons on the instrument panel, but Dr. Gebhart had not answered his question about the lever at the far right. He had shown Herbert how the rocket was to be blasted off by pressing a button on the outside of the tower. Herbert had had sense enough to leave *that* button alone.

What Dr. Gebhart had not told Herbert was that the highly concentrated fuel which would send the rocket into space could be ignited from inside the rocket as well as outside. How was Herbert to know that there was more than one way to send the rocket into space? How was he to know that the lever to the far right of the

instrument panel would ignite the highly concentrated fuel?

"It's the same distance from the center to the
lever on the far right as it is to the one on the far
left, which releases a banana pellet," thought
Herbert. "Maybe pressing the one to the right
will send out a cherry-flavored pellet. It would
do no harm to find out," Herbert decided. So,
yielding to curiosity, Herbert firmly pressed the
lever at the far right of the instrument panel.

A blinding flash was followed by a deafening
roar. Up went the rocket with Herbert aboard.
With unbelievable speed, the rocket zoomed
through the atmosphere on its way into outer
space.

Herbert began to whistle to keep up his courage. Whistling had always helped him from
feeling scared. Then, he remembered that Uncle Horace had shown great confidence in Dr.
Gebhart, having given him large sums of money
for research and for building the rocket. "If Uncle Horace believes in his ability, why shouldn't
I?" thought Herbert, and his whistling became
more cheerful.

"The Russians sent the first dog into space,
but I bet I'm the first boy," he thought.

It was thrilling to look out the rocket porthole and see mountains, rivers, oceans, and continents grow distant and then disappear.

"Here I go into the high blue yonder," sang Herbert, off key. By this time, he was feeling pleasantly excited.

Just about now, however, Herbert was conscious of great bodily heaviness. "I feel as if I weigh a ton," he thought. "But it won't last forever," he encouraged himself, remembering what he had read about flights by astronauts.

What a relief it was when the heaviness was gone! Soon, instead of feeling that he weighed a ton, more or less, Herbert had the sensation of being nearly as light as air.

Wanting to get the full effect of this weightlessness, Herbert unbuckled the padded straps of his contour seat. Then, he had to put out his hands quickly to avoid bumping his head on the ceiling of the cockpit.

"It's a little like being like a balloon with nobody holding on to the string," thought Herbert. Then he enjoyed turning somersaults, standing on his head, and other feats which would have been difficult, if not impossible, if he had not been so nearly weightless.

Finally, feeling a bit lightheaded as well as weightless, Herbert succeeded in strapping himself in the contour chair again.

Now, outside the port, he could see velvety blackness pierced with brilliant stars. Flecks of brightness were falling past the port, like sparks from a skyrocket.

Feeling hungry, Herbert pushed the lever which released the banana pellets and ate twelve. He wished they came in other flavors. He also had a drink of water from a tube attached to the instrument panel and connected with a small tank.

"Good-by, world. Be seeing you," Herbert said to the now far-distant earth. He wondered where the rocket was aimed and remembered that Dr. Gebhart had said it was going in the general direction of Mars. Well, he would know when he got there, wherever that might be, he reasoned.

He suddenly felt sleepy. After all, he had been up hours earlier than usual. "I don't know where I'm going, but I'm on my way," he thought drowsily, and fell asleep.

4

"I'll Be Doggoned!"

Herbert had awakened so early that morning that he had sleep to make up, so it was all of twelve hours before he opened his eyes again. "Where on Earth am I?" he thought before he remembered that he was not on Earth at all but was hurtling through outer space farther and faster than man or beast had ever gone before.

After yawning and stretching (and he found it a bit difficult to stretch while wearing a space suit), Herbert realized that he was hungry and thirsty. He had another drink of water (he wished it were milk, nice cold milk) and ate four more banana pellets. By this time, Herbert was very sick of the taste of bananas and was sorry that apples had not been Susy's favorite food instead. Herbert was pretty sure he would not have lost his appetite as soon for apple pellets.

Feeling cramped from being in the same seat for so long, Herbert unloosened his seat straps and tried to do a few exercises. But he found it impossible to do push-ups while weightless, and cracked his head on the ceiling of the cockpit when he attempted to do knee-bends.

"I'll just have to forget physical fitness for the time being," he thought as he fastened himself in his contour seat again.

Through the port, he watched the stars. Herbert grew a little bored with seeing stars. He wished that a comet might appear, but apparently it was the wrong season for comets. No brightness with a long tail flashed by the porthole. After a while, for want of anything better to do, he went to sleep again.

He was in the midst of a dream in which he was giving a daring performance on a flying trapeze (one of Herbert's last year's ambitions) when he woke up with a jerk. The circus ring abruptly faded from his mind's eye. With great

excitement, he realized that the rocket was no longer in motion. While he had been asleep, it must have reached its destination. But what was that loud pounding against the side of the rocket?

"Stop!" shouted Herbert. "You'll smash the rocket."

Apparently, he was not heard, for the deafening pounding continued. *Bang*! *Bang*! *Bang*!

Herbert felt responsible for Dr. Gebhart's rocket. Besides, if it were wrecked, how would he ever return to Earth? Herbert had no desire to make this a one-way trip into space. Knowing that the automatic pilot had been set to return to Earth had made him less worried during the flight than he might have been otherwise.

Hurriedly, Herbert unfastened his seat belt as, through the port, he saw that the rocket had put down its slim landing legs in a field. Herbert was glad the rocket had come down on land not sea, but he had to put a stop to that pounding against the side of the rocket. Some inhabitant of this strange planet was trying to smash through the rocket's shell near the air lock. Herbert could feel the vibration from the powerful blows even from the opposite side of the cockpit. He rushed over and pressed the buttons which unlocked both the inner and the outer doors.

While Herbert was in the small airtight compartment which separated the inner from the outer door, he undid his space suit enough so he could reach in his pocket for his Boy Scout knife. Quickly, he pulled out two blades and the corkscrew. Then he opened the outer door.

Herbert saw that a tall ladder had been placed on the side of the rocket, and not a human but a huge dog had been striking heavy blows against the side of the rocket close to the door. The big dog was wielding the most enormous sledge hammer Herbert had ever seen.

"Cut that out," bawled Herbert. Then, seeing that there was a living being on this strange planet, which proved there must be air to breathe, Herbert took off his space helmet in order to make himself heard. "Stop that pounding. Do you hear me? Quit it or I'll —"

Herbert had no chance to prove what he would do if the big dog (a boxer by its head) did not obey him. A long, hairy arm reached out and grabbed Herbert and, in spite of his kicking and struggling, he was carried down the

54

ladder. All the way down the ladder, the boxer kept up a ferocious barking, which was answered, from below, by other excited barking. Herbert's threats and yells were quite drowned out by the din.

Two bulldogs (Herbert could tell they were bulldogs by their heads) rushed up to Herbert. They, like Herbert's captor, were wearing robes of thin material belted at as much of a waist as a dog has. All three dogs wore high boots of something which looked softer than leather. They all stood upright like men and their forepaws had separations which were elongated into fingers of a sort.

Herbert, however, was too intent on getting back to the rocket to pay much attention to the appearance of the huge dogs. He made another attempt to make himself understood, speaking slowly and making gestures.

"I can't stay away from the rocket," he said, "for I don't know when the automatic pilot is set to take off." Then, deciding to try friendliness, he stopped kicking and struggling, and said pleasantly, "I am fond of dogs and most of them are fond of me. I have a dog named Mortimer. Mortimer is one of my best friends." And

how Herbert wished that Mortimer were here to talk dog language to these outsized dogs!

The dogs paid no more attention to Herbert than men do to the jabbering of monkeys. They went on barking, but less loudly and in a more conversational manner. Herbert could tell that he was being barked about as they examined him with curious eyes and with not ungentle paws.

One of the bulldogs (the one wearing a green robe) hurried away. The boxer still kept a grip on Herbert that was tight as a vise but did not actually hurt him. The tallest bulldog (he was twice the size of an ordinary bulldog) took Herbert's knife from him and examined it, holding it in his pawlike hand or handlike paw (Herbert could not decide which to call it). Closing the blades and the corkscrew, the dog gave the knife back to Herbert. Herbert would have pulled the blade out again and tried to stab his way to freedom if the boxer had not been holding his right arm so tightly. Herbert was very right-handed and knew he could do little effective stabbing with his left.

In spite of his resentment at being held on to like a newly captured criminal, Herbert gazed with interest at his surroundings. The field where the rocket had landed was on a rise of land just outside a walled city. Through a wide gate less than a hundred feet away, Herbert could see trees, roads, and houses not unlike those on earth, although all the houses in sight seemed to be made of curiously shining stones of varied colors.

Herbert wondered what the inhabitants of this strange planet looked like. Were they like the odd-looking beings Herbert had seen on TV programs as the inhabitants of Mars? Herbert had seen a program on color TV in which men from Mars had green faces. Of course, this might not be Mars, though Herbert remembered hearing Dr. Gebhart say that the rocket was going in its general direction. And, of course, the TV story writers had only guessed what men from Mars might look like.

"Maybe I'll be the one to find out for sure," thought Herbert, and looked around for somebody looking at least nearly human. But all he saw were dogs.

A car came out through the wide gate and drove over the field. "Over" was the right word, for the car had no wheels and its body was above the ground by a full foot. Herbert had heard that cars of the future would float above the ground, but he was astonished to see one here. "The inhabitants of this planet must be smart," he thought. Then he saw that no Martian-looking being was at the wheel of the car. A bulldog wearing a green robe was at the wheel, the same bulldog who had left so hurriedly after Herbert's capture.

"Dogs certainly are smart here, too," thought Herbert. "When I get back to Earth, I'll try to teach Mortimer to drive. Or I would if I were old enough to drive myself."

Despite Herbert's struggles, the boxer holding on to him lifted Herbert into the back of the car. The two bulldogs sat in front. Herbert kept hoping that the boxer would relax his hold. When he did, Herbert planned to jump out of the car and run back to the rocket as fast as he could leg it. The ladder was still in place, and Herbert would climb it and fling it down before the dogs could capture him again. Then, Herbert would press that lever to the right and blast off. Or so he hoped.

The big boxer, however, did not relax his hold. The car passed through the wide gates at which Airedale sentries stood on guard. The gates were closed.

"These dogs don't understand a word of English, but I hope and pray their masters do," thought Herbert as the car drove along a tree-lined avenue. "I have to make somebody understand that I have to get back to the rocket in a hurry. I'll tell them I'd love to stay longer but I don't know exactly when the automatic pilot is set to start the rocket back to Earth."

But still Herbert saw no human or even near-human beings. Big dogs on moving sidewalks stood on each side of a busy street. There were spaniels, collies, German shepherds, terriers, Dalmatians, poodles, setters, hounds, and several breeds unfamiliar to Herbert. All the dogs were walking on their hind legs and were wearing clothes.

Herbert saw lady dogs wearing high-heeled sandals and gazing in shop windows. He saw dogs with briefcases coming out of office buildings, dogs coming out of bookstores — dogs and more dogs. Even puppy dogs were being pushed in baby carriages by dog nursemaids. And car after car had a dog driver.

As the car Herbert was in neared the center

of the city, the suspicion Herbert first had on seeing so many dogs driving cars became a certainty. Intelligent life on this planet had taken a different shape from man.

"I'll be doggoned!" cried Herbert aloud. "All the inhabitants of this planet must be dogs."

Hearing him speak, the big boxer patted Herbert with his free paw. His intelligent brown eyes were kind. He was a good dog, Herbert decided, civilized and not at all savage. But how was Herbert going to make him understand that he must return to the rocket at once? That there was no time to lose.

As Herbert was again pleading and still not making himself understood, there was a roar as loud as a clap of thunder. Herbert looked back and saw the rocket whoosh into the air, trailing a tail of flame. The automatic pilot had evidently been set to take over at this moment and was now guiding Dr. Gebhart's rocket back to Earth. Without Herbert!

5

At The Zoo

Herbert had been in tight places before, but always, in case of need, Uncle Horace had come to the rescue. But Uncle Horace was now worlds away. There was no way, this time, to send word for him to come at once. Still, if the automatic pilot did take the rocket safely back to Earth, Dr. Gebhart would surely notify Uncle Horace that his favorite nephew was stranded on a strange planet. Then, if the rocket had made one successful trip, why could it not make two? Herbert hoped that Uncle Horace, and not Susy, the chimpanzee, would come after him.

It was bound to be some time, however, before anybody would come after him, Herbert reasoned, as the car sped on. In the meantime, he would find out all he could about this strange planet where the intelligent form of life was dogs. Herbert did not let his mind dwell on the possibility that something might go wrong with the rocket and he would be forced to lead a dog's life the rest of his days. For it was not Herbert's nature to look on the dark rather than the bright side of life.

After passing through the main street of the business district, the car Herbert was in floated around a corner to the right and entered a park. Herbert saw happy puppies riding a merry-go-round and small dogs digging in a sand pile. Even the small dogs were larger than Mortimer and, although they all looked like dogs, they acted like people. Their barks sounded as much like a foreign language as they did like the barking of dogs on earth.

The car had not gone more than a mile through the park, when Herbert's nose made him suspect that, besides being a playground, this park was a zoo. Then he not only smelled but saw wild animals as the car passed cage after cage. Herbert caught a glimpse of a giant lizard

which looked like a dragon in a storybook. In another big cage there was an animal which he thought might be part elephant and part zebra, for it was the size and shape of an elephant yet had stripes like a zebra. In another cage, monkey-like creatures were playing.

"Could be that Susy would feel more at home on this planet than I do," mused Herbert. Then he wished the car had slowed down so he could have had a better look at an extremely large and fierce-looking lion, angrily pacing its cage.

The car stopped at a long, low building. With the boxer still holding on to him, Herbert entered the building. The two bulldogs stayed behind in the car. The boxer knocked at a door opening from the corridor, and a smooth-haired terrier came to the door. He stepped back in fright and astonishment at the sight of Herbert, ·yet he did not try to prevent Herbert and the boxer from coming into a large, pleasant room.

Two lady greyhounds stopped typing, their eyes wide with amazement not untinged with fear. But the large Newfoundland wearing glasses, who got up from his desk, showed interest and surprise yet did not seem especially afraid of Herbert. Herbert could tell that the boxer and the Newfoundland were holding an animated barking about him.

Herbert judged that the Newfoundland must have pressed a button as he got up from his desk for two bloodhounds rushed in. Instead of the robes Herbert had seen the other dogs wearing, the bloodhounds wore trouser-like garments which looked like extra wide-legged blue dungarees. One of the bloodhounds carried a rope and whip and the other a stout chair. They kept some distance from Herbert but did not take their eyes off him for an instant. They acted as if they thought Herbert were a dangerous wild animal.

"How ridiculous!" thought Herbert, but he was unable to prove that he was not a wild animal because he still could not make himself understood, either by words or gestures.

A tall dog carrying a doctor's satchel now came running in. He was of no breed of dog Herbert recognized. He looked to Herbert to be a mongrel with a strong strain of wolf, and Herbert took an instant dislike to him. That was partly because Herbert saw contempt in the doctor-dog's eyes, and Herbert was not accustomed to being looked at as a lower form of life.

The doctor-dog now proceeded to give Herbert a physical examination, with all the dogs present looking on with great interest. Not being able to hear Herbert's heart through his space suit, the doctor-dog ordered the boxer who had captured Herbert to take it off. The boxer was gentle about removing the space suit. Yet he was careful to keep out of the way of Herbert's mouth, in case he might bite.

Then the bloodhounds stood on guard with whip and chair while the doctor-dog listened to Herbert's heart and lungs through a stethoscope. He also felt Herbert's pulse, took his temperature, and poked and prodded him, even after Herbert said "Ouch." The doctor did not seem to mind if he did hurt, and Herbert disliked him more than ever for that. Herbert had always been fond of dogs, but he knew he could never be a friend to this one.

"What this place needs is not a society for the prevention of cruelty to animals but a society for the prevention of cruelty to humans," muttered Herbert, after a particularly hard pinch. But, of course, he was not understood. The doctor-dog went on examining Herbert for several more minutes. The expression in the doctor's eyes was of cold intelligence, curiosity, and revulsion. So might a scientist on earth examine a new species of disagreeable bug.

The examination over, the doctor-dog and the Newfoundland held a spirited argument. Herbert sensed it was about him and that there was a difference of opinion about what should be done with him. Herbert was relieved that apparently the Newfoundland won the argument, for the doctor-dog gave a snarl indicating disappointment, picked up his satchel, and left, slamming the door.

"He's a bad-tempered cur if ever I saw one," thought Herbert. "Now what?" he wondered.

What happened to Herbert next, he found even more unpleasant than the physical examination. The two husky bloodhounds, under the supervision of the Newfoundland and the boxer who had captured Herbert, herded him out of the building and into a cage on a large truck. The cage was shut and locked, and the truck driven to a secluded spot in the park where there was an especially roomy cage. Then Herbert was shifted, in spite of his protests, from the cage on the truck to the larger cage in the zoo.

"I'm no wild animal," Herbert shouted. "I'm as smart as any of you super-dogs, or whatever you are. Maybe smarter." It was no use. He was not hurt nor roughly handled, yet he could not prevent his being put in the cage. Four strong dogs, with several others running up to help, were too many for Herbert to fight. Outraged and helpless, Herbert found himself caged in the zoo like a wild animal.

"Men on earth wouldn't treat a dog like this," shouted Herbert, shaking the bars. "Let me out of here. Let me out."

The zoo keepers just stood outside and gawked at him. And the boxer who had captured Herbert at the rocket barked soothingly before he went away.

The cage, as large as a good-sized room, was furnished with bars to swing on, a tree to climb, and an overhanging slab of rock which formed a cave. Hay was piled on the floor of the cave. In a trough surrounding the cage was clear running water. Here were all the comforts of home for almost any wild animal, but Herbert was no wild animal. It made him furious to be considered a strange species, fit only for a zoo.

Two zoo keepers brought food to him. Not knowing what this newest acquisition to their zoo was used to as a diet, they brought great hunks of meat, both raw and cooked. There was also a head of cabbage and a half-loaf of bread and several varieties of fruit. After placing these on his feeding tray, one of the zoo keepers poured out a measure of oats and forked in some fresh hay. "What do you think I am, a horse?" shouted Herbert.

The bloodhound zoo keeper did not answer. He backed away carefully while his assistant stood ready to protect him.

Herbert thought he was too angry to want to eat, but he scooped up water in his hands to quench his thirst. Then he decided he had better eat to keep up his strength, so he ate some of the cooked meat and part of the half-loaf of bread. His appetite grew after the first few bites, so he had quite a good meal. For dessert, he ate a fruit somewhat like an apple and another somewhat like a pear. He did not touch the fruit which was somewhat like a banana. After all those banana pellets during his voyage through space, Herbert did not care if he never saw another banana again — or any fruit which even faintly resembled one.

Herbert felt slightly less discouraged after having had something to eat. When, however, dogs of every species known to man, besides a few others, came to see the strange creature from outer space, Herbert hid in the cave and would not come out. Herbert usually enjoyed being the center of all eyes, but not under these circumstances. He did not like being looked at as a curious but inferior species. He was relieved when it was closing time for the zoo and the crowd of dogs in front of his cage had left.

Darkness came after a short twilight. The animal noises in the zoo were louder after dark. The roars, howls, bellows, and bleatings, did not frighten Herbert, but he'd had a hard day and was tired and sleepy.

"Pipe down. I want to go to sleep," he shouted, but the zoo animals understood no more English than the super-dogs. Lying on his bed of hay in the cave, a bed no harder than many he had slept on during overnight Boy Scout hikes, Herbert fell asleep to the harsh music of the snarls of tigers and lions and the throaty coughing of nearby sea lions. His last waking thoughts were of home. He hoped his family was not too worried about him. He hoped Uncle Horace had been notified about what had happened to him. He hoped he would be able to show the dog inhabitants of this planet that he was an intelligent being and not a wild animal. He hoped to return to Earth in the not too distant future. So, only a little worried and discouraged, Herbert hopefully went to sleep. Not even the loudest of the animal noises disturbed his dreams.

6

Herbert Makes A Friend

Herbert was awakened the next morning by a sneeze, as a wisp of hay tickled his nose. For an instant, he thought himself in a haymow he had once slept in on an overnight Boy Scout hike. Then he came wide awake and saw sunshine through the bars of his cage. But the sunshine did not cheer him. He was still furious at being kept a prisoner behind bars in a zoo. He was still outraged at being considered a lower form of life than a dog.

"Somehow, I've got to get out of this zoo," thought Herbert. But he had not come up with any definite plan when the bloodhound zoo keeper brought him his breakfast.

The zoo keeper, seeming more friendly than frightened, actually got up courage enough to pat Herbert on the head. Herbert had never liked being patted, especially on the head, but he thought it best to conceal his displeasure.

"At least, you've apparently decided I won't bite," Herbert said to the friendly bloodhound. "Guess you've concluded I'm a tame not a wild animal. But I sure wish I knew a way to get it through your thick head that I don't belong in a zoo."

Of course, the zoo keeper did not understand Herbert, but he looked so pleasant that Herbert was tempted to pat *him* but refrained, thinking that zoo keepers might not like being patted by the zoo inmates.

Herbert always felt better-natured after breakfast than before, and this morning was no exception. When the gates of the zoo were opened and hordes of dogs streamed in, Herbert did not hide in the cave as he had the day before. As long as so many dogs had come to the zoo with the express purpose of seeing him, Herbert was willing to be seen.

Soon, inspired by the wide-eyed interest and

admiration of his spectators, Herbert put on quite a show for them. He stood on his head, did gymnastic exercises, chinned himself on the bar in his cage, and turned handsprings and somersaults. All this so delighted the dogs outside Herbert's cage that bulldog policemen had difficulty in keeping them moving. And it was necessary that the dogs be kept moving, for dogs were lined up half a mile beyond the zoo entrance, waiting to see this strange creature from outer space.

"If they have circuses on this planet and a circus manager comes by, maybe he'll buy me from the zoo to do tricks in his circus," thought Herbert, standing on his head and sticking his tongue out at the same time, which any boy knows is difficult. But would life as a trained human in a circus be any better than living in a cage at the zoo? Herbert had no way of knowing, but he continued putting on a performance to pass away the time. Besides, he found himself enjoying the obvious pleasure on so many doggy faces.

"I'm wowing them," thought Herbert, waving at a puppy as he rested from more strenuous exercises.

Herbert came upright from walking on his hands across the cage and saw a handsome young collie gazing at him, not only with interest and admiration but with longing. Herbert was reminded of how he had stood outside a pet shop window and yearned to own the puppy who became his dog, Mortimer. It was a new experience for Herbert to be wanted by a dog. He was not sure he liked it. The collie lingered until told to move on but, an hour later, Herbert saw him again in front of the cage.

"That dog," thought Herbert, "is a repeater." And this time, Herbert was a little sorry to see the young super-dog go away, for somehow the look of affection in the handsome collie's dark eyes made Herbert feel less lonely on this strange planet where dogs walked like men, and a human being was thought to be lower in intelligence than a dog. At least, here was a super-dog who liked Herbert.

So, the morning passed. Around noon (Herbert judged it was noon by the sun), a zoo keeper came with a hose to wash out Herbert's cage. Not wanting to get wet, Herbert moved to the far corner, and there stood the young collie outside the cage again. For the third time, he had waited in line to see Herbert. Herbert was touched by the young dog's devotion, and he returned the collie's bark of greeting with a broad smile.

Just then, a short distance away, there were excited yelps and barks. Down the path which led past the cage ran two Dalmatians, a gray poodle, and a Husky. Chasing them was the enormous lion Herbert had glimpsed when he had been brought into the zoo.

The line of dogs around Herbert's cage milled about in confusion. Mother dogs snatched up their puppies and ran for their lives. The young collie did not have time to run. He had been so engrossed in gazing at Herbert that he had not turned to see the lion coming. Now the lion was almost upon him.

If the lion had not paused to roar, Herbert would not have had time to act. As fast as he had ever run in his life, Herbert raced across the cage and snatched the hose from the zoo keeper. Fortunately, the hose nozzle was similar to those on Earth. Herbert turned on the water full force. As the lion crouched to spring, Herbert hit the beast right between the eyes with a strong stream of water. Herbert's being a crack shot with a water pistol helped his aim.

By this time, four zoo keepers with long poles came on the run. One of them carried great hunks of raw meat, which he threw at the enraged beast. Herbert did not turn off the water until he saw the lion surrounded and then shot with a tranquilizer. Soon, the lion was peacefully eating the meat and, in a few minutes, allowed himself to be driven back to his cage. Herbert never did learn how the lion had gotten out of his cage.

Now the dogs around the cage barked their gratitude to Herbert for having saved their lives. Of course, Herbert could not translate their barks into English, but he could read the expression of gratitude on their faces. Nobody seemed as grateful — or had as much reason for being grateful — as the young collie. He looked at Herbert as if he really loved him.

Herbert did no more stunts to amuse the dogs the rest of the day. He behaved as he thought a hero should — with dignity. Now and then, he bowed and smiled as the admiring dogs passed by his cage.

"They ought to give me a medal for this," Herbert thought, turning on a smile for a trio of Dalmatian puppies. "What I did should have proved that I am at least as smart as a dog, even a super-dog." And Herbert kept expecting somebody to come and let him out of his cage.

It was nearly closing time for the zoo when Herbert saw the dogs near his cage step back to allow three dogs to come to the door. One of them was the Newfoundland Herbert had rightly assumed to be the director of the zoo. The other two were collies. They looked so much alike that it was obvious they were father and son. The younger of the two was the young collie who had taken such a great liking to Herbert. In spite of the bars between them, the feeling had been mutual. Herbert was happy that he had been able to save this handsome young collie from being mauled, and perhaps killed, by the fierce lion. (Later, Herbert was to learn that the reason the lion had been so fierce that day was because he had been suffering from a toothache.)

The zoo director unlocked the door of the cage and the three dogs entered. The young collie rushed up and embraced Herbert, barking happily.

"Now I have convinced the dogs that I, too, am an intelligent being. They have come to set me free. They will probably treat me like a hero," thought Herbert. But his high spirits were dashed when the zoo director put a collar studded with green stones around Herbert's neck and gave the leash to the young collie.

"They think I'm smart for a being that's not a dog, but still inferior," thought Herbert, much disappointed. He remembered that, on Earth, dogs had been given medals for saving lives, but nobody afterwards had considered them man's equal. Apparently, it was the same here in reverse.

Proudly, the young collie led Herbert from the cage and down the path to a waiting car. The chauffeur, a red setter, whose ears, like those of Uncle Horace's chauffeur, Mike, looked chewed but not recently, opened and closed the car door in the back and took his place in the driver's seat up front. Herbert sat between the two collies.

The zoo director bowed to the young collie's father and waved as the cars started. The young collie and Herbert waved back. Herbert was glad to be leaving the zoo. Being at a zoo, he had learned, was more pleasant when you were outside a cage, not in one. But Herbert, although happy to be out of a cage, was not reconciled to having a collar around his neck.

After a short drive, the big car floated up a curving driveway and stopped in front of a fine house larger than the city hall in Herbert's town back home. A butler dog (a short-haired terrier) opened the door and seemed reluctant to let Herbert come in. Herbert could tell that the young collie was having quite an argument about it. But Herbert was let in and was led into a spacious and elegantly furnished room where the young collie's mother was playing the piano. She stopped playing and there was some excited barking between the three collies.

Herbert knew that she had been told about what had happened at the zoo when she smiled at him and patted him on the head. Herbert was getting very bored with being patted on the head, but he sensed that she meant well and that it was her way of thanking him for saving her son's life.

That night, Herbert was given his dinner in a dish on the kitchen floor. The cook (an Irish terrier) acted scared of Herbert and kept her distance. Herbert was tempted to act ferocious, since she seemed to expect him to be both fierce and wild, but he decided it was wiser to act tame. It hurt his pride to eat with his fingers from a dish on the floor, but he was hungry and the food was good — much better than the food at the zoo. Every servant in the house (all terriers) came to look at Herbert eating his dinner with his fingers from a dish on the floor.

After dinner, the young collie took Herbert for a run in the extensive grounds. He surprised Herbert by being able to run on his two legs faster than Herbert could. After a few races (and the young collie good-naturedly let Herbert win the last), the boy and the dog played ball with a large rubber-like ball. The young collie threw the ball and obviously expected Herbert to go fetch it. He looked astonished but pleased to see Herbert pick up the ball and throw it back. The collie could catch a ball either in his mouth or in his paw, which Herbert thought clever of him. Dog and boy played ball until bedtime.

Herbert was glad that he was not put outdoors for the night but was allowed to share the collie's bedroom. As were all the other rooms in the house, the bedroom was beautifully furnished, but there was no bed in it, just a large puffed silk mat for the collie to sleep on and a smaller mat for Herbert beside it.

Herbert was slow in getting to sleep. Being in this fine house was a great improvement on being kept behind bars in a zoo, but Herbert knew he never could be resigned to being regarded as inferior to a dog, no matter how kindly he might be treated.

"Someway, I must convince these super-dogs that I am an intelligent being," Herbert vowed. But he still could not figure out how he could do this. "Who on Earth," he thought, as he was drifting off to sleep, "would ever have dreamed that I would be a pet boy to a dog?"

7

Break-through

Herbert woke up the next morning determined to prove to the collies that he was not just a tame animal but a civilized being. When Prince (Herbert called the young collie Prince because he lived in a house like a palace and had something princely about his character) took his human to the kitchen for his breakfast, Herbert refused to eat from a dish on the floor. He picked up the dish, took it to the kitchen table, got out a knife, fork, and spoon from the drawer where he had noticed they were kept, and drew up a chair and sat down. He was more careful about his table manners than he sometimes was at home because he wanted to make an especially good impression.

Pleased and astonished at this show of civilized behavior, Prince ran to get his parents to come and see Herbert eating his breakfast like a super-dog. They also were pleased and astonished. Before they had finished barking about it, however, it was time for Prince to go to school, and the first of the twelve eminent doctor-dogs and scientists coming to study Herbert was at the door.

Prince's father waited until the twelve eminent doctor-dogs and scientists were seated in his spacious library before he led Herbert in. He motioned Herbert to a chair, and all the very eminent doctors and scientists were surprised to see an animal of a strange species sitting in a chair. They all looked pleased as well as surprised, except the mean-eyed mongrel who had examined Herbert at the zoo. He growled deep in his throat, and the look in his eye would have frightened Herbert, if Herbert had been easily frightened.

"I'm glad the zoo director did not let *you* take me home, you bad-tempered, evil-eyed, surly, ill-begotten cur," Herbert said to the

wolfish-looking dog, and perhaps it was fortunate for Herbert that his words were not understood by any dog there.

In a kindly manner, Prince's father made Herbert understand that he was to submit to a thorough examination by the twelve eminent doctor-dogs and scientists. The contents of Herbert's pockets had been taken from him at the zoo, but had been returned when the collies took him home with them. Now each item was passed from paw to paw and scrutinized with great care. There was a stick of gum, the wrapper from a candy bar, a jackknife, a piece of chalk, a shark's tooth, a pencil with a broken point, three marbles, a paperback baseball handbook, and a dime and three pennies. The eminent doctors and scientists were especially interested in the dime and three pennies, and took turns looking at them through a microscope.

Then Herbert had to undergo another physical examination. None of it hurt until the wolfish-dog jabbed him cruelly with a blunt instrument and pricked him with a sharp one. He also flashed an intense bright light in Herbert's eyes. He was just getting a pair of pincers out of his doctor's bag when Prince's father strenuously objected. Apparently, the noble-faced collie was king-dog around here, for the doctor-dog sullenly put the pincers back in his bag.

Herbert had known and had liked several mongrels back on Earth, but to this one he had taken an instant dislike, which was obviously mutual.

"I don't know what your name is, but I'll call you Dr. Wolf, for you look as mean as a wolf, if not meaner," thought Herbert.

Herbert did not object, however, when Dr. Wolf and all the other eminent doctors and scientists got out cameras to take pictures of him. Herbert never objected to having his picture taken. He said "cheese" a few times so some of the pictures would show him smiling, frowned so others would show him frowning, and stuck out his tongue for variety when one picture was snapped.

After the picture-taking, the eminent doctors and scientists made tape recordings of Herbert's voice. When Herbert was made to understand what was expected of him, he obliged by reciting all he remembered of Lincoln's Gettysburg

Address, gave the salute to the flag while standing at attention, and gave one word for each letter of the alphabet, hesitating only over a word beginning with z before he remembered zero.

Herbert was almost out of breath by then, but he rested only a moment before reciting four television commercials, counted up to five hundred by fives, and said the multiplication tables beginning with the ones and ending with the sixes. And, by then, Herbert really was just about out of breath.

When urged to continue, Herbert sang the Marine Hymn, always a favorite of his, and, deciding that he had been serious long enough and that doggerel was appropriate to recite to dogs, he spoke a silly poem he had recently learned.

> *"I wish I were a little egg,*
> *Away up in a tree,*
> *Rocked about by every breeze,*
> *And rotten as can be.*
> *And then I wish some little boy*
> *Would climb up after me.*
> *I'd up and bust my little self,*
> *And spatter him with me."*

Herbert knew that "bust" was not good grammar, but he thought that, since the dogs did not understand the words, it did not matter. Of course, nobody but Herbert found the verse funny.

By this time, Herbert was tired of tape recording and was relieved that nothing more in that line was expected of him.

While all this examination had been going on, all the doctors and eminent scientists had been taking notes. Now Herbert was able to make one of them (a handsome greyhound) understand that he wanted a piece of note paper. The greyhound gave Herbert a pencil and paper and he and the other doctors and scientists intently watched what Herbert did with them.

First Herbert tried to express himself in pictures. He was no artist, but he really exerted himself. He drew the almost round globe of Earth and a stick figure representing himself seated in the cockpit of a rocket flying in space. Then he drew the rocket landing and stick dogs capturing him.

"This will show you that I remember what

happened to me," Herbert said, passing the paper around.

Then Herbert wrote a short note to his Uncle Horace.

Dear Uncle Horace:

I wish you were here. This is an interesting planet, but one might say that I have gone to the dogs.

Your loving nephew,
Herbert

This used up the sheet of note paper and Herbert passed the letter around.

"This will show you that I know how to write," Herbert told the eminent doctors and scientists, who, with the exception of Dr. Wolf, looked impressed but not yet convinced that Herbert was a civilized being.

Herbert next picked up the paperback baseball handbook and began to read from it.

He read aloud that the New York Yankees had been champions in the American League far more often than any other team. He read a list of home-run leaders. "Babe Ruth," he read, "hit sixty home runs in the year 1927." Then he read a long list of no-hitters, and the number of perfect games pitched in major league championship play from 1880 to the previous baseball season. "Now you know that I can read," said Herbert, closing the paperback baseball handbook.

All the eminent doctors and scientists, with the exception of Dr. Wolf, looked impressed and almost convinced that Herbert was an intelligent being. Herbert realized, however, that he still had not quite convinced them.

Herbert searched his mind for some further means of communication. If only he could find a bridge between the two cultures — something which would be the same on both planets. His eye fell on a large clock on the wall. It was not unlike clocks on earth except that the numbers denoting the hours were different. Herbert's mind raced as he came up with an idea.

Again, Herbert made it known that he wanted paper and a writing implement, which were given to him. Sitting down at the library table facing the clock, Herbert drew a clock face. Only, instead of copying the numbers as they were on the clock here, Herbert wrote the clock numbers from one to twelve, like those on

clocks on Earth. Then he drew another clock face and carefully copied the numbers on the large library clock. The next step was to list the numbers in two rows, with a 12 matching a corresponding number, according to the large library clock.

Rapidly, Herbert did a few simple sums in arithmetic, never using a number above twelve. He then wrote down the answers both in the numbers he was accustomed to using and the numbers used on the dog planet.

Herbert passed this paper around and every dog examined it. Then dog after dog rose to his feet and made a speech. Herbert could tell that they were speeches about him and that most of them were admiring and flattering. Only Dr. Wolf still looked unimpressed. He made an angry speech and seemed to be in disagreement with every other dog there.

When all the dogs had finished speaking, Prince's father did something which would have made Herbert weep for joy if he had been a weeping-for-joy boy. The noble-faced collie un-buckled and removed the collar from Herbert's neck. Then he cordially reached out a paw and shook Herbert's hand while every dog there (with the exception of Dr. Wolf) applauded by clapping their paws vigorously.

Herbert could tell that he must have convinced the super-dogs that he was an intelligent being. And, he was thankful that, from that time on, he would not be wearing a dog collar.

8

Herbert's Diary

After having been accepted as an intelligent being by all the super-dogs, except the mongrel Dr. Wolf, Herbert was treated by Prince and his parents as one of the family. But, since Herbert's lack of knowledge of the dog language made communication difficult for him (though Herbert was getting to be skillful at making himself understood by gestures), Prince's father engaged a tutor for Herbert. A dignified German shepherd came five mornings a week to teach Herbert the language of the dog planet.

Herbert's teachers on Earth would have been astonished to see how hard Herbert studied.

But if he wanted to converse with the super-dogs (and Herbert always liked to talk), he knew he had to learn their language. By means of phonograph records, pictures, gestures, the pointing out of objects and the repeating of their names, and above all, because of the patient teaching of his tutor, Herbert made rapid progress in learning the dog language.

Prince was a great help. He never minded repeating the names of objects, though he sometimes smiled at — but never actually made fun of — Herbert's mistakes.

What with morning-long sessions of tutoring and hour-long afternoon conferences with visiting dignitaries, scientists, doctors, and newspaper men, Herbert had little idle time. Two afternoons a week, bus loads of school puppies were brought to see this strange specimen of life from another planet. As each puppy passed in single file, Herbert shook his or her paw. For those small dogs too timid to extend a paw, Herbert had a friendly pat and a reassuring smile. It was a proud day for him when he was able to greet them and to say good-by in dog language.

In a matter of weeks, the tutor, as well as Herbert, had further reason to be proud, for Herbert was able to address an audience of eminent scientists and educators in dog language. He tried to describe life on Earth to them, but since his vocabulary in dog language was still limited, he had to say what he knew how to say and not all he would have liked to have said. His efforts, however, were generously applauded.

Herbert remembered that Arctic and Antarctic explorers, and other discoverers of new lands on Earth, often kept diaries in which they recorded the weather, meetings with strange tribes, and other observations they felt would be of interest. So, Herbert decided to do the same. Maybe after he got back to Earth (and Herbert had by no means given up hope of getting back to Earth), some publisher might want to print Herbert's diary. In his mind's eye, Herbert could already see LIFE ON THE DOG PLANET by HERBERT YADON on a book cover. Herbert thought he would choose to have the cover either red or green — he rather favored red.

Here are Herbert's entries for the week of July 12-18, after he had been on the dog planet nearly four weeks.

July 12. It rained for the first time since I have been here. Rainfall is controlled and it only rains when a poll shows that a majority of super-dogs feels that rain is needed. The super-dogs do not have umbrellas. If caught in the rain, they just put on dry clothes and throw away their wet ones. Clothing is so cheap, it is only worn one day and can be bought in vending machines. Male and female dogs dress alike except that the robes of the lady dogs have ruffles. Workmen wear blue jeans over their robes, only you can't really call them *blue* jeans because they are sometimes green or pink or some other color.

July 13. Sunny and pleasant. The temperature on this planet is also controlled, but I haven't yet found out how that is done. I'm not dead sure, but I think it never snows here. Can't be sure of that unless I am still here during the winter, and I'd rather not be here that long. Wish there were some way of letting my folks know I am okay. Hope Pete, Donny, and Chuck are over their chicken pox.

July 14. Sunny and a little cooler than yesterday. Went to visit an art museum with Prince. He's some dog. Treats me like a brother. Better than some brothers treat their brothers. In one room of the museum there are portraits of famous super-dogs. The largest portrait is of Prince's great-grandfather, a famous warrior. It seems that this city was nearly conquered by wolves years ago, and Prince's great-grandfather led the army which defeated them. There are still wolves outside the walls of the city, Prince says. That is why there are guards at intervals along the wall and electrified wires at the top.

July 15. Cloudy and cool but not too cool. The super-dogs like variety in their weather, but so far, there has been no fog. Visited another museum and saw my space suit on exhibit. Hope I can get it back when I need it again. The curator of the museum says it is the most popular exhibit there. Dog biscuits are better here than on Earth. I once ate one of Mortimer's and didn't like it. Wish Mortimer were here, only it might hurt his feelings to find so many dogs smarter than he is. He also might get tired if he tried to walk on his hind legs all the time.

Well, to come back to dog biscuits. I like best the ones which taste like chocolate chip cookies with nuts and some that are like our sugar cookies sprinkled with caraway seeds. The gingerbread dogs aren't bad, either. Cooking is much faster here than on Earth. Cookies bake in one minute — you just put them in, press a button, and take them out. It takes three minutes to roast a roast over ten pounds. Four if you like it well-done.

July 16. I should have described the geography of this place before. Some of the facts I've only known recently. I'm on a planet much, much smaller than Earth. Probably that's why there's nothing about it in the astronomy books. I'm not dead sure, but I think it's not much bigger than the state of Ohio. It is inhabited by dogs in a high state of civilization and by wolves and wild dogs who are still barbarians. The city I am in is the capital city of the super-dogs, as I call them. A wall with an electrified fence surrounds the entire country belonging to the super-dogs. Not just this city as I first thought. The wall was built after the super-dogs conquered the wolves. My rocket landed in wolf country, but I didn't see any wolves. Prince says that most of them live on the other side of a mountain that is east of the city. I wanted to visit the spot where the rocket landed, but the guard at the gate wouldn't let me. He said that nobody is allowed outside the wall except under extraordinary circumstances. Apparently, I was an extraordinary circumstance the day I landed but am no longer considered one. Prince's father is top dog or ruler of this country. Where I live is his palace. I didn't know it was a palace at first, because I thought palaces have towers, but I may have been thinking of castles. Besides reception rooms for dignitaries in the palace, Prince's father has a large suite of offices downtown in the city hall.

July 17. Dr. Wolf came to see Prince's father. He presented a petition signed by his friends (and he's so mean, I don't see how he can have many) asking that I be turned over to him for intensive scientific study. I'd about as soon be skinned alive, in fact that's what might happen to me if I got in his clutches. He's a bad dog. He still insists that I am a lower form of life than dogs. He doesn't like Prince's father,

either. He writes letters to the newspapers com-
plaining about him. Prince thinks Dr. Wolf
would like to have his father deposed (that
means kicked out). If Dr. Wolf were a dog on
Earth, I'd be glad to have the dog catcher catch
him. He is the doctor who was so rough when
he gave me a physical examination soon after I
landed on this planet. Whenever we happen to
meet, he growls at me and I growl right back. I
can now growl exactly like a super-dog. Dr.
Wolf should be watched. Prince's father tore
up the petition.

July 18. Sunny and breezy. Prince had a
holiday from school because it was the anniver-
sary of the day his great-grandfather conquered
the wolves. I went with Prince to an industrial
exhibit. I saw a number of gadgets we don't yet
have on Earth. You can talk to some tools and
they work without your touching them. I saw
a hammer pound nails and a screwdriver screw
screws with nobody holding on to the handles,
which are shorter than the handles of tools on
Earth. But the dogs' inventions get out of order
sometimes, just as ours do. Prince and I watched
a mechanical servant demonstrate how to keep

house. It did all right the first time it was set to perform. It washed dishes, swept the floor, and polished furniture. But, when we stayed for a second demonstration, something got mixed up in its insides, for it swept the window with a broom, put furniture polish on the dishes, and scrubbed the furniture with window cleaner. Prince says his father will keep live servants until the mechanical ones are perfected. Super-dogs do not wear hats. That may be because most of them have sticking up or long, floppy ears.

Herbert was less regular about writing in his diary after that week, but he never failed to record the weather. He also listed the flora and fauna of the planet, which he knew meant plant and animal life. Herbert had never kept a diary nearly as long before. Usually, he stopped writing in a new diary after a few days. But now he had things to describe which had never been described before, not even by Jules Verne. Herbert felt it his duty to tell the world about them, and he still dreamed of having his diary published as a book with a bright green or, preferably, red cover.

9

Baseball

Although Herbert was learning the language of the dog planet rapidly, even after a month, Prince's father felt he would make faster progress at home with a tutor than going to school with Prince. Herbert was always sorry to see Prince start off to school without him, for he had become very fond of the young collie. Sometimes, Herbert found himself liking Prince so much that he felt a bit disloyal to Mortimer. He had always liked Mortimer better than any other dog. But, of course, Prince was another *kind* of dog.

Herbert was relieved when the eminent doctors and scientists stopped making their daily visits, and he was also glad when the bus loads of puppies were scheduled to come once a week instead of twice. Now, although he still worked hard at learning the dog language, Herbert had more leisure time.

Since Herbert was no longer so busy, Prince began to bring his classmates home from school to play. The young super-dogs were all good-natured, and soon Herbert did not feel at all strange playing with them. They ran races and Herbert was chagrined that all but a dachshund could beat him. At swimming — the collies had a large swimming pool — Herbert and the dogs were about evenly matched. Herbert, however, was a shade better at diving, perhaps because he had a more tapered shape.

The principal sports on the dog planet, Herbert learned, were racing (both by car and on foot), swimming, bowling, boating, and bird watching. No baseball. Herbert could hardly believe it possible that any living creature, either in inner or outer space, did not even *know* about baseball, let alone how to play the game.

"I'll have to do something about that," Herbert thought, and he decided to begin by teaching Prince and his classmates how to play sandlot, if not regulation, baseball. But there was, of course, no baseball diamond, no bats, no baseball gloves, and only softballs a little larger than regulation baseballs. "We certainly will have to start from scratch," Herbert wanted to tell Prince, but since he did not know the word for *scratch* in dog language, he had to say, "We must start from almost nothing," which meant about the same thing.

After Herbert had described the game to him, Prince became most enthusiastic, although he did not take in the fine points of the game. But Herbert made him understand that they must have bats and drew a picture of one. He also drew in chalk on a cement walk a diagram of a baseball field.

"We'll get the head gardener to help us," Prince said, after he understood that the diagram was merely a diagram and not where the game was to be played. "And the gardener's brother is a good carpenter. He can make us those sticks you hit the ball with."

The palace grounds out back, which were the most level, certainly changed in appearance during the next few days. Two trees were sawed down and their stumps pulled, four flowering shrubs were moved, and an oval bed of geranium-like flowers transplanted. The head gardener, a Scotty, did most of the work with the help of the assistant gardener. He only grumbled when Herbert, Prince, and Prince's playmates helped after school. Herbert did not do any of the actual sawing, digging, or transplanting. He supervised the work, for he was the only one who knew what a baseball diamond looked like.

Even though the palace grounds were spacious, there was room for only a junior-size baseball diamond.

"We don't really need an outfield," Herbert told Prince.

Prince was not sure what an outfield was, but he agreed, being a good-natured dog and having confidence in Herbert.

The head gardener's brother, under Herbert's supervision, made a sample bat exactly the right size for Herbert to swing. It would also do for a dachshund and a cocker spaniel, who were good friends of Prince's. Bigger bats had to be made for the larger dogs. The head carpenter's brother made twelve bats of assorted sizes, and Herbert was pretty sure that would do for a start. He figured it did not matter too much that they had no catchers' mitts and gloves since the balls they would play with were soft, and the dogs caught balls as easily in their mouths as in their paws. Either way of catching was okay with Herbert, for he did not believe in being too fussy.

Now came the task of teaching the dogs how to play baseball. And was that a job to do single-handed! Before the first practice was half over, Herbert was hoarse from yelling and his legs ached from running here, there, and everywhere on the baseball diamond.

Since there were no baseball terms in dog language, Herbert found it difficult to make himself understood. Instead of "Batter up!" he had to take the proper position and say, "He who tries to hit the ball with the stick stands here and swings at the ball like this." And Herbert motioned to Prince on the pitcher's mound to throw a ball which he hit, with a satisfying crack of the bat. In a real game, that would be good for three bases if not a home run, thought

Herbert. But he realized why the ball had been so easy to hit.

"How many times have I told you not to aim at the stick?" he scolded Prince. "You're supposed to get the ball over the plate, yet not let the dog with the stick hit it."

"I thought a plate was something you ate food from," Herbert heard the bulldog catcher remark.

Herbert sighed. He had forgotten that a word in dog language can have only one meaning. But what could you call it, if not *plate*? Even Herbert's brain was tired by the time they finished that first baseball practice. Trying to make the dogs see the difference between a ball and a strike, how to steal bases, and how far the batter had to bat the ball to make a safe run to the home plate — all this was exhausting, especially since Herbert had to act out all the plays. But the dogs loved it. They assured Herbert that they would play baseball every afternoon as soon as school was out. But Herbert, weary as he was, wondered if it had been such a good idea to introduce baseball to the dog planet.

By the end of several days of practice, however, the twelve dogs (six to each team, since they did not have outfielders and the basemen could double for them) showed great improvement, although Herbert realized that they were still not as good as any Little Leaguers he had seen play. They did not even play as good ball as Pete, Donny, Chuck, two fourth graders, and a small but eager first grader often played on a vacant lot back home. Thinking of playing ball on the vacant lot near his house made Herbert feel a bit homesick. If he had not had so much to occupy his mind, he might have been *really* homesick and worried. For he had expected that Dr. Gebhart would have sent the rocket back after him long before this. But, he would not let his mind dwell on the possibility (he never acknowledged that it might be the probability) that the rocket might never return.

A week after they had begun baseball practice, Prince came home with news for Herbert. As part of the celebration of the next holiday, which was Prince's father's birthday, Prince had invited his entire school, including the teachers and principal, to attend a baseball game.

"And the principal is asking the School Board, and my father is inviting a number of eminent doctors, scientists, government officials, and newspaper men to come, too," said Prince happily.

"But we're nowhere near ready to play an exhibition game," cried Herbert.

"Everybody has already accepted the invitations," said Prince. Then he put a comforting paw on Herbert's shoulder. "Don't worry," he said. "Nobody but my father, who has watched us a few times from his library window, knows a thing about the game, so they won't recognize a mistake if they see one."

"They're likely to see more than one," said Herbert. "We have only one more day to practice before we put on the show."

Prince's father asked the weather man to consult Herbert about the weather he wanted the day of the exhibition game. Herbert requested a sunny but coolish day with no wind. Herbert knew what a strong wind could do to a baseball.

The game was set for three o'clock in the afternoon and, by two-thirty, the spectators were taking their seats on the bleachers the head gardener, the assistant gardener, and the head gardener's brother, who was a good carpenter, had finished building only an hour before the game was to begin.

Exactly on the dot of three o'clock, Herbert faced the bleachers and gave a brief explanation of the game of baseball, hitting only the high spots, of course. He was sorry to see that most of the spectators looked puzzled when he had ended his brief speech. Somehow, he doubted if many there would become real baseball fans. "But you never can tell before a game," he thought hopefully.

It was to be a five-inning game, for Herbert was afraid his players couldn't last the usual nine, and he was pretty sure he couldn't. For Herbert had to be combination coach, score-keeper, and umpire, which kept him on the run most of the time. He stood part of the time behind and a little to the left of the pitcher to call balls and strikes. Yet, he sometimes judged if a ball went over the plate or not from a position near third base, where he had raced to signal dogs on bases if it were safe to steal. His decisions had to be quick and convincing, and all the time, he kept up a stream of instruction, rebuke, and words of encouragement.

What a ball game it was! Prince pitched for

his team and a southpaw Airedale for the other. The players were of assorted sizes, the largest was twice Herbert's size and the smallest not as tall. A dachshund on Prince's team and a cocker spaniel on the Airedale's made the teams about equal in the size of the players. But, of course,

Herbert knew that it is skill not size that counts in baseball. Bulldogs caught for both teams, their jaws being particularly adapted for catching, though they had ready paws as well.

Prince was first on the pitcher's mound. In his excitement, he forgot and aimed at the bat and allowed three hits before Herbert chewed him out and he tightened up. But not before the Airedale's side had scored. In the second half of the first, in spite of being put off by southpaw pitching, Prince's team played good ball. Herbert hid his joy (wanting to appear impartial) when Prince hit a beautiful line drive and romped home. It was one to one for the first inning.

In the second inning, the first dog up clouted a curve ball that came over too slow. He made it to second base, stole to third when the next dog up popped a fly, and came home on the next hit. Then Prince tightened up, and the side was retired with no further score. But the Airedale's side was now one ahead.

With batters up for Prince's side, his team got excited and swung at any ball pitched, whether it went over the plate or not. Their bats fanned the air more often than they connected with the ball. One dog dodged every ball instead of swinging at it. Herbert bawled him out for that. He also told the Airedale pitcher, in no uncertain terms, to stop aiming his fast balls at the batter's head. The side was retired with no score for Prince's team. The other team was still ahead.

In the third and fourth innings, the playing got wild. Dogs on bases got so interested in watching the pitching that they forgot to steal bases, even when signaled that it was safe. Herbert was dismayed when there was a pile-up of three dogs on first, and there were so many errors that he gave up calling them. The fourth ended with a score of seven to six, with the Airedale's team still one ahead.

Both teams were tired by the fifth inning. So was Herbert. Prince was on the pitcher's mound still trying, but he gave a walk to the first dog up. Then he was faced with the best hitter of the other side, a handsome Dalmatian who had scored two of his team's runs.

Prince's jaw was set with determination. He pitched his fastest ball. Strike one. Then a sinker made it strike two. A beautiful curve ball, and the Dalmatian was out.

But Prince's arm was tired, and the hits he allowed the next two batters filled the bases. Only a happy catch by the second baseman retired the side without a run.

Now Prince's side had their last chance at bat. A Husky hit a grounder which got him to second base. He stole third, and another hit brought him home. That tied the score. But two dogs had struck out when the dachshund picked up his bat.

"Here goes the ball game for Prince's side," thought Herbert, for the dachshund had struck out his two times at bat.

Crack went the bat. To his surprise, as well as everybody else's, the dachshund hit a beauty far down center field. The ball rolled, which was a help to him. But it was the speed of his small legs going like pistons that brought him home, with all his teammates and every spectator not related to the other team cheering like mad. Prince's team had won the game.

Herbert congratulated both teams. "You played real baseball," he said, and thought he could be forgiven for a slight exaggeration.

The spectators were all enthusiastic. They had, to a dog, become baseball fans.

"I hope you'll invite us to another game soon," super-dog after super-dog told Herbert.

Herbert was so tired, he felt right now that he could never live through another ball game. But he was still polite.

"The next game we play, except for practice games, you'll have an invitation," he promised.

Herbert might have scheduled another ball game soon if he had not suddenly thought of introducing another activity to the dog planet. With Prince and his playmates, who were by now Herbert's playmates, too, he would form a Boy Scout troop. Only, of course, here it would be called a Dog Scout troop. Herbert, naturally, would be the scoutmaster, and he hoped that his troop would be only the beginning of an extensive scouting program on the dog planet.

"Boys like belonging to the scouts, so why shouldn't dogs?" Herbert reasoned.

10

Dog Scouts

Herbert's scoutmaster back home was a retired master sergeant by the name of Timothy
Tuttle. Herbert could not make his voice sound
as gruff as the sergeant's, but it came natural to
him to snap commands in the same manner.
Often wishing that he had brought along his
Boy Scout handbook as well as the baseball
handbook, Herbert taught the dogs scouting
from memory.

Herbert could not remember, for sure, how
many knots a beginning scout is supposed to
know how to tie, but he taught the troop how
to tie seven, including the carrick bend. He also

showed them how to give artificial respiration, light a fire without matches (the dogs had matches though they seldom used them since their heat and light were automatic), stop bleeding if it were not too severe, and to communicate a few words in Indian sign language. Herbert decided against teaching the dogs the deaf-and-dumb alphabet, since their paws, although as useful as human hands, did not have what you could really call fingers.

Herbert would have taught the dogs how to identify the birds, trees, and minerals of the planet, only the dogs already knew much more about them than Herbert. He got around that by giving the scouts merit badges for teaching *him* to identify twenty birds, sixteen trees, and ten minerals found there. Herbert designed the merit badges, and Prince's mother hired a tailor to make them. They had a red background (red being Herbert's favorite color) and blue, green, and yellow insignia. The blue was for skills; the green for collecting living objects such as bugs, butterflies, and harmless snakes and toads; and the yellow was for collecting lifeless things such as sea shells, rocks, minerals, and fossils. Apparently, there were no sea shells or fossils on the dog planet, at least, no collections had been made of them.

"Maybe that's because no dog has looked hard enough for them," declared Herbert.

One late afternoon, Herbert, Prince, and a young dachshund Herbert called Frank, because he was so much the shape of a frankfurter, went out to dig for fossils or almost anything interesting their trowel-shaped implements might turn up. They chose a hill not far from the barrier between the wolf country and the dog kingdom as a likely place for finding fossils, if they could be found anywhere. But they dug and dug and found none. Prince, however, was pleased to find two spearheads.

"They must be from the spears that dog warriors carried in their victorious battle against the wolves," said Prince. "That was the army my great-grandfather commanded," he reminded the others. Prince was a modest dog, but he certainly was proud of his late great-grandfather.

"I'll present them to the Museum of Natural History," said Prince, clearing the dirt from the spearheads. "The museum is always interested in adding historical objects to their collection. They also will accept any unusual rocks or animals. Of course, if we should find an unusual animal which is not too wild, I'd probably want to keep it for a pet instead of having it killed and stuffed for the museum."

Herbert remembered seeing the exhibit of stuffed animals at the Museum of Natural History. On one of the exhibit cases was the name of the donor. In dog language, the name meant "Most Learned Doctor," but Herbert knew him as Dr. Wolf.

"I think it would please Dr. Wolf to have me killed and stuffed and put on exhibit in the Museum of Natural History," said Herbert.

Prince laughed. "He is a stubborn dog," he said. "He still insists that you act from instinct not reason, and is still furious that my father has refused to let him make further tests on you. Dr. Wolf is ridiculous. No living being would know how to play baseball instinctively, to say nothing of the other abilities you have shown. I knew the first time I laid eyes on you that you were an intelligent being."

"Then why did you let your father put a collar around my neck and keep it there until I proved my intelligence?" Herbert thought, but refrained from asking. "Race you to the top of the hill," he cried instead. "Come on. Get set. Go!"

Off they ran and Prince, as usual, won. The dachshund came in last but did not mind. He was a very good-natured dog, and Herbert liked him almost as well as he did Prince.

From the top of the hill, they could see the fields outside the city. They could also see a portion of the electrified fence separating the dog kingdom from the country of the barbarian wolves. There was no guard in sight.

"Last week, my father's council voted to reduce the number of guards," said Prince. "It is true that the wolves have given us no trouble for a long time. Dr. Wolf made a most eloquent speech in which he said that guarding against danger when no danger is present is a waste of dog power."

"Say," cried Herbert. "I think I see a wolf down there on the other side of the fence. And there's a dog on this side talking to him."

Prince and Frank both looked, but their eyesight was not as keen as Herbert's.

"I think you're seeing things," said Prince.

"I really do see a dog and a wolf on opposite sides of the fence," insisted Herbert. They were too far distant for him to be sure, but something about the dog, even when seen from the distance, reminded him of Dr. Wolf. Yet, Herbert acknowledged that he may just have had Dr. Wolf on his mind. All the way home, however, Herbert felt vaguely worried and could not figure out the reason why.

Herbert did more for his scout troop than go collecting with them. He taught them to shoot with bow and arrow. It was a sport new to the dog planet, though they were expert at spear throwing, javelin hurling, and an odd sport in which dogs on stilts ran relay races.

Herbert persuaded the assistant gardener's brother to make two bows and several arrows. That dog was a whizz at following Herbert's sketches and directions. Then Herbert drew a target with a bull's-eye on a barrelhead and nailed it to a tree near the junior-size baseball diamond. When the dogs were not practicing baseball, they tried their skill at archery. They took to the new sport with enthusiasm and were soon so good at it that Herbert gave all the scouts in the troop merit badges for proficiency in archery.

After two weeks' experience in scouting, Herbert felt his troop was ready for an overnight camping trip. Camping not being one of the customs of the super-dogs, there were no tents available, but Herbert said they could make adequate tents out of old blankets.

"They'll do fine if it doesn't rain," said Herbert at the meeting called to make plans for the overnight hike.

"I'm quite sure the polls call for fair weather, but I can ask my father to make a special request as he did for the baseball game," said Prince.

"Good! Now, each scout will need to bring two blankets — one for his half of the tent and the other for bedclothes," Herbert instructed the dog troop.

It turned out that the dog troop needed only two tents, each sleeping two, for some parents were timid about letting their sons go on an overnight hike in Herbert's charge. The parents may have been influenced by a letter Dr. Wolf had written recently to the leading newspaper. In the letter, he accused Herbert of introducing alien sports to the dog planet and of being a harmful influence on young dogs. "Except as a subject for scientific research, this creature from outer space should not be allowed to exist on our planet," the letter ended. Only the dachshund, Frank, and a bulldog nicknamed Smiley, because of his wide grin, turned up to go with Prince and Herbert on the overnight camping trip.

After a long walk, the campers pitched their tents at the foot of a hill near a spring. Herbert pronounced a flat ledge in front of the two tents to be the perfect spot for a campfire.

"Next thing is to go after firewood," said Herbert. "Get dry wood if you can, it burns better. We'll need a lot of wood. Got to have enough to cook our dinner and still keep the fire going for hours."

"Why do we need a fire after we've cooked our dinner?" asked Prince.

"For storytelling and singing around the campfire," Herbert answered. "We always did that on our overnight hikes at home."

"You tell the stories and do the singing," said Prince. "I don't have much of a voice for singing."

Frank and Smiley said they didn't have much of a voice for singing, either.

"Well, neither do I," confessed Herbert, "but we can do a little howling in unison, and I'll teach you the words of a camping song I know. But what are we hanging around here for? We've got to get wood."

Prince, Smiley, and Frank went up the slope of the hill looking for firewood. Herbert hunted for deadwood at the foot of the hill. Here the electrified fence was almost hidden in shrubbery. Years ago, trees had been cut down; probably, Herbert thought, when the fence was first put up. It was a fine place for gathering deadwood.

Herbert had an armful of wood when he came upon a hollow log.

"Gosh, that must have been a big tree!" he thought. "Looks big enough for a man to crawl through. Anyway, a boy. Think I'll try it." He put down his armful of wood and went in the log, feet first.

Once inside the hollow log, Herbert was worried for a few seconds when he got stuck in the middle and seemed unable to go forward or back. Then, by drawing in his breath and pushing with both hands and feet, he came out sneezing his head off because of the dust from the rotten wood.

Herbert thought the hollow log would be fine for the campfire. They could shove it in a little at a time and it would last a long while. But it was too heavy for Herbert to move alone.

Herbert was about to call to the other scouts to come and help him, when he stepped back toward the electrified fence and almost fell into a hole. He turned around quickly and looked up. One wire had been cut. And the hole was under the fence, below the cut wire, a hole large enough for a wolf to crawl through.

"Prince, Frank, Smiley! Come here quick," he yelled. "Hurry!" And there had never been more urgency in Herbert's voice.

It was plain to Herbert that the wolves must be planning a surprise attack on the dog kingdom. Even now, they might be massing their best fighters on the other side of the fence. At any minute, the first attackers might come crawling through that hole under the fence.

"We've got to stop them. But how?" Herbert wondered. Yet, by the time Prince, Frank, and Smiley had joined him, Herbert had a plan.

He cut short the dogs' expressions of astonishment, outrage, and dismay.

"Prince, you're the fastest runner," said Herbert. "Run as you've never run before back to town and give the alarm. Get to your father or the chief of police. Have them send soldiers, guards, police dogs. Anybody with a weapon. Go!"

Prince was off like a shot. He was only a few steps away before Herbert had the other dogs helping him drag the hollow log over to the hole under the fence. They turned it until the hole at one end of the log matched the hole under the fence. Then Herbert sent Smiley for the biggest rock he could bring or roll.

"You go back to the camp site and bring back the baseball bat and bow and arrows we brought along," Herbert ordered Frank. "Get them here in a hurry."

While Frank ran back to the camp site, Herbert stood at the end of the hollow log inside the fence. He had a stick in his hand, ready to strike any wolf who might emerge. A baseball bat would make a stronger weapon, but Herbert was prepared to put up a fight with anything at hand.

Frank was back in almost no time. Both Herbert and Frank could now hear the horrid howling and snarling of wolves on the other side of the fence.

"You're a good shot with the bow and arrow," Herbert praised Frank, seeing that the dachshund looked a little scared. "You stand far enough away to get a good aim. I'll stand nearer so I can hit any wolf coming out of the log over the head with my baseball bat. I'll clobber them. Hope they come out head first, not feet. But I'll hit anything that comes out of that log. When Smiley gets back with a big rock, we'll use it to plug this end of the log. That'll slow them down. By that time, Prince should be back with help."

Herbert spoke more hopefully than he felt, for he was afraid it would be some time before Prince could get back. "Good thing we brought a baseball bat and a bow and arrows along so we could get in some practice," Herbert thought, swinging his bat to get his arm loosened up.

Minutes passed and no wolf appeared — head or feet first. Then there was a fierce burst of howling. Herbert would have found it nerve-racking, only his nerves were not easily racked.

"They've discovered that end of the hollow log," Herbert said in a low voice to Frank.

In another minute, Herbert heard movement in the hollow log. He stood at his end of it, bat poised. The noise stopped.

"He's stuck. Hope he's stuck for good," thought Herbert. But the noise soon began again. "He's got himself unstuck," thought Herbert, and wondered how strong a blow it took to stun a wolf.

Now an ugly snout appeared. "Not quite yet. There's not enough to hit," Herbert told himself. Then, as the whole ugly head emerged, Herbert gave a mighty swing with his bat. And the howl of pain that wolf gave was deafening. Herbert got in another blow, and the huge, hairy beast lay motionless half in and half out of the hollow log.

Just then, Frank let loose an arrow that Herbert barely dodged in time.

"Hold it," cried Herbert. And that was the time Smiley appeared rolling a big boulder.

It took the three of them to pull the unconscious wolf entirely out of the log. Herbert was

glad he had rope enough in his pocket to tie him up, in case he came to. Then, Herbert helped Frank and Smiley plug the end of the hollow log with the big rock. And all the time, the howling and snarling on the other side of the fence was growing louder.

"We've got 'em worried," cried Herbert happily. Then he was the worried one. He could hear the wolves digging another hole under the fence.

Herbert with his bat, Frank with his bow (he still had two arrows left), and Smiley, with a pile of loose rocks beside him to throw at the wolves, stationed themselves where the sound of digging was coming from. Herbert was thankful that stones in the way apparently kept slowing down the digging. He would have been happier if the wolves had had to dig through solid ledge.

Herbert kept up a stream of encouraging words to his companions. He said, "We'll show 'em. We're not afraid of the big, bad wolves," and similar remarks. But Herbert was very relieved when soldiers, guards, Prince, dignitaries, and electricians to mend the fence came swarming down the hill!

So, once again, the dog country was saved from the wolves, and this time Herbert was given most of the credit.

"I did no more than Prince, Frank, and Smiley," Herbert said modestly several times. But he knew he really had done more, and accepted the role of hero with pleasure.

Herbert shook the paw of so many grateful dignitaries that his hand was sore. One expression of gratitude especially pleased him. Prince's father said he was engaging a sculptor to make a statue of Herbert.

"You will be posed with that stick you hit a ball with in your right paw," said Prince's father. "And the statue will be erected in City Hall Square. I shall suggest a ten-foot statue, at least."

It pleased Herbert that the sculptor would be making the statue more than life-size.

11

Captured

It was the opinion of Prince's father and his advisers that the wolves must have been planning their attack for some time. Herbert could not forget the dog he had seen at the electrified fence ten days or so before the attempted attack. Had it been Dr. Wolf, and was he conspiring with the wolves to lead an attack against his country? Herbert talked to Prince about his suspicions and Prince told them to his father.

Prince's father said that, although he disliked Dr. Wolf, he had no reason to suspect him of unpatriotic motives. And, after all, Herbert had no proof. The wolf Herbert had captured would not talk, although the dogs understood the language of the wolves, which was more primitive than that of the dogs. The captured wolf was in jail waiting to be tried and sentenced. Just thinking of the ugly, hairy beast he had hit over the head with his baseball bat made Herbert shudder. For, although the wolves on this planet had reached a higher development than wolves on Earth, they were fiercer and uglier besides being much larger.

Every day, Herbert went to the sculptor's studio to pose for his statue. On pleasant days, he walked, for the sculptor, a great Dane, had his studio not more than half a mile from the palace. The studio was set back from the highway and almost surrounded by tall trees. The private road leading to the studio was like a country lane, seemingly quite apart from the busy city.

Although it was hard for Herbert to sit still for long periods of time, he rather enjoyed posing for his statue. It was a pleasure to see his likeness — several times its natural size — emerging from white marble. The great Dane devoted all his time to working on the statue. By the end of ten days, he had roughed out the body and was making remarkable progress on the head. He told Herbert that, after one more sitting, he could finish without needing Herbert to pose again.

The afternoon of his last sitting, Herbert stayed a little later than usual, for the sculptor celebrated the occasion of his last session of posing by serving refreshments. There was a soft drink something like a coke with a strong citrous fruit flavor and the most delicious dog-biscuit cookies Herbert had ever tasted. They not only had nuts in them but were iced.

It was dusk when Herbert said good-by to the genial great Dane. As he walked between two rows of trees toward the highway, Herbert was wondering if it would be possible, with the help of the assistant gardener's brother, to set up a basketball court and teach his scout troop how to play.

"There's a vacant room in the palace basement which would be big enough," Herbert thought. "I think —" But Herbert did no more thinking along that line. From behind a tree, a tall dog darted out and flung a cloth over

Herbert's head. Herbert was conscious of a pungent, sweetish smell. Before he could snatch the cloth away or call for help, he lost consciousness.

When Herbert came to, he found himself in a large cage. The cage was in a brightly lighted white-tiled room not unlike an over-sized bathroom or a moderately-sized laboratory. It had one barred window, and about the room were several large pieces of apparatus.

"Looks like the therapy room of a doctor's office," thought Herbert, putting his hand to his aching head because the potent anesthetic had left his head aching. "Who's done this to me?" he asked himself, but he was not greatly surprised when Dr. Wolf came into the room and stood in front of the cage. For only Herbert's worst enemy would have captured him, and Dr. Wolf was Herbert's *only* enemy on the dog planet. Now Herbert realized that he was at Dr. Wolf's mercy, a quality Herbert was pretty sure the mongrel doctor did not have.

"In case you are wondering where you are," said Dr. Wolf in a sneering voice, "you are in my cellar laboratory, a place where I carry on intensive and secret research. I anticipate learning a great deal about your species before I am done with you. Then, if my political plans for this country are not again thwarted, I shall, with pleasure, have you stuffed and put on exhibit in the Museum of Natural History."

"It *was* you I saw that day talking to a wolf," accused Herbert. "I've suspected you of treason ever since."

"Fortunately, you alone suspected me," said Dr. Wolf. "Yes, it was I who conspired with the wolves to attack the city. I was to be the new king. And shall be yet," he said, his eyes glaring, "though it will be more difficult now that the guards at the barrier have been doubled. The wolves blame you for that. If I followed their counsel, I would throw you to them immediately. I wish, however, to make an exhaustive study of a sub-canine species, so have brought you here. You might have found it less painful to have been thrown to the wolves, but some sacrifice has to be made for the advancement of science." The look of cruelty in Dr. Wolf's eyes was frightening.

"You can't get away with it. I'll be rescued," cried Herbert. "As soon as I'm missed, the police will be out searching for me."

"They will not think to look for you here,"
said Dr. Wolf. "Nobody knows the existence of
this cellar laboratory."

"They'll find me. Dogs can track by their
sense of smell."

"An attribute the inhabitants of this country
have not possessed since prehistoric times," said
Dr. Wolf. He walked to the door and, on his
way out, switched off the lights, leaving Herbert
in total darkness.

Herbert had been in tight places before but
never in as much danger of losing his life as
now. Of course, once, several years ago, he had
been in danger of being scalped by the Indians.
Uncle Horace had come to his rescue then. But
maybe the Indians were scaring him and would
not have really scalped him. "Oh, Uncle Horace, if you only knew how much I need your
help now," thought Herbert. But, this time, he
knew he could not count on Uncle Horace's
help.

Herbert was not one to give up without a
struggle. He tried to bend the bars of his cage.
They would not bend. He thought of trying to
dig his way to freedom through the floor, but
his touch told him that it was made of a hard ce-

ment-like substance, impossible to dig through. Besides, Herbert had nothing to dig with, having given his scout knife to Prince weeks before as a token of friendship.

In spite of his natural optimism, Herbert's thoughts were dark in the long, lonely hours before he sank into a sleep of exhaustion. He dreamed that he was racing down Tunlaw Street with his friends Pete, Donny, and Chuck just behind him. His dog, Mortimer, was running beside him barking at the top of his lungs.

"Pipe down, Mortimer. You'll disturb the neighbors," Herbert said in his dream. Then he came awake, and the barking was no dream. And there was little similarity between that barking and the language of the civilized dogs. It sounded like Mortimer's bark, and Herbert thought he would know Mortimer's bark anywhere.

"Mortimer!" yelled Herbert. "Here I am. Mortimer!"

Herbert saw a light flash at the laboratory window. "Help! Help!" he screamed.

There was the rasping sound of the window bars being cut. And, all the time, the barking went on.

"It can't be Mortimer. It can't be," Herbert told himself. But it *was* Mortimer. As soon as there was space enough between the bars, Mortimer jumped into the laboratory and dashed to Herbert's cage in a frenzy of joyous barking. It was one of the happiest moments of Herbert's life when he felt Mortimer's tongue licking his hand.

Mortimer was soon followed by guards, by Prince, policemen, and several members of the Dog Scout troop. Then (and by this time the lights had been turned on) Uncle Horace himself stepped, in his dignified manner, first to a chair and then to the floor of the laboratory.

"Herbert, I am very glad to see you," he said, shaking hands with Herbert through the bars of his cage. "We'll have you out of here in no time. But it's Mortimer you can thank for bringing us to you. It was Mortimer who followed your scent and led us here."

A bulldog policeman easily picked the lock outside the cage, and Herbert rushed out and hugged Mortimer hard while Prince was hugging him.

"Dr. Wolf is under arrest. He has confessed all," said Prince. "And the rocket you came in to this planet landed again not more than two hours ago. The few words you taught me in your language let me understand that this dignified being (and he meant Uncle Horace, not Mortimer) is related to you. He was as anxious as I to find you."

"Maybe more so," thought Herbert, but did not think it polite to speak his thought aloud.

Cars were waiting to take Herbert, Uncle Horace, Mortimer, and the super-dogs back to the palace. Herbert was gratified that the car he and Uncle Horace and Mortimer were in had a police escort.

Uncle Horace and Herbert had a great deal to say to each other. Uncle Horace explained that, when the rocket had returned to earth without Herbert, he had persuaded Dr. Gebhart to let him make the same charted flight in the hopes of finding his nephew.

"You took your time about coming after me," said Herbert.

"The delay was necessary because the rocket needed minor repairs before making another flight," said Uncle Horace. "I brought Mortimer with me because he has done nothing but mope since you left home. By the way, I gave your parents the impression that you have been spending your summer vacation with me. That was to save them worry."

"Good," said Herbert. "I'm glad *they* haven't worried."

"Well, *I* have been worried about you," scolded Uncle Horace. "When Dr. Gebhart telephoned me that you had taken the chimpanzee's place in the trial flight, I was much disturbed. You really should not have taken off that way, Herbert."

"It was an accident," said Herbert, and told his uncle about pressing the wrong button.

"It was impulsive action on your part as well as an accident," scolded Uncle Horace.

At the palace, Prince's parents invited the entire Dog Scout troop to have a late supper with Herbert and his Uncle Horace. Herbert was happy to serve as interpreter, and translated polite phrases both for his uncle and the superdogs.

It was a joyful occasion for everybody there except Mortimer. Herbert could tell that Mortimer felt ill at ease among these big dogs who walked on their hind legs, ate their food sitting at a table and with knives, forks, and spoons, and conversed in a language Mortimer could not understand. Nor could the super-dogs understand Mortimer's barks any more than Herbert could understand monkey talk, which was not at all. Herbert patted Mortimer from time to time so he would not feel neglected.

Supper over, Uncle Horace looked at his watch. "The automatic pilot is set so the rocket will be taking off in less than an hour," he said. "I cannot express my gratitude to you for your kind treatment of my nephew," he told Prince's parents. "Now, as a last favor, I must ask you to have us driven out to the rocket."

Of course, Herbert did the translating of these remarks.

"Must you go, Herbert?" pleaded Prince.

"Can't I take Prince home with me?" Herbert begged his uncle.

Uncle Horace shook his head.

Herbert could understand that Prince might not be happy in a land where the dogs were so much inferior to him.

"I'll be back," Herbert promised Prince. "I do hope I can come back sometime soon."

"It can't be soon enough," Prince said, real affection in his fine dark eyes.

Prince and his parents drove Herbert, Uncle Horace, Mortimer, and the entire Dog Scout troop out to where the rocket had landed, this time within the dog country. As they passed City Hall Square, Herbert remembered his statue which was to stand there after it was finished.

"A statue of me, more than twice my size, is to stand right there," he told his uncle.

"That's just fine," said Uncle Horace, but his mind seemed more on the rocket than on Herbert's statue. "I hope the timer for the automatic pilot isn't fast," he said, and he breathed a sigh of relief when he could see that the rocket was still there. Flares had been set around the rocket so it was visible for some distance.

Soon the last good-bys were said and Uncle Horace, Herbert, and Mortimer were in the rocket putting on their space suits. Herbert's had been brought from the museum by order of Prince's father, another example of his thoughtfulness. Of course, Herbert had to do the putting on of Mortimer's space suit. He was glad to be doing it inside the rocket cockpit so the super-dogs could not see that Mortimer was not in the habit of dressing himself.

Herbert was not sure, but he hoped that Prince could see him wave from the port when the rocket blasted off with a whish and a roar.

"I've really had a nice time, but I'm glad to be on my way home," said Herbert to Uncle Horace.

12

Back To Earth

With Uncle Horace with him, Herbert was not at all worried for fear the rocket might not return to earth. He was pleased, too, that his uncle had brought along no banana pellets to eat. Instead, there was soup, chopped-up meat and vegetables to be squeezed through tubes, and delicious soft custard and creamy milk chocolate. Of course, Herbert was not hungry during the first part of the flight, having had such a good meal at the palace before leaving the dog planet.

Herbert and Uncle Horace still had a lot to say to each other during the flight, though at first Uncle Horace did more listening than talking. Herbert's feelings were slightly hurt when his uncle was more amused than indignant at hearing that his nephew, on his arrival on the dog planet, had been put in the zoo.

"I have sometimes thought that a zoo might be the proper place in which to keep growing boys," said Uncle Horace.

Herbert was not amused although he knew his uncle was joking.

"I can't get over how fluently you learned to bark," said Uncle Horace. "But why couldn't Mortimer understand those super-dogs?"

"Because they don't bark in the same language," said Herbert. "There is as much — if not more — difference between Mortimer's barking and Prince's as there is between the way men and monkeys talk."

"I understand," said Uncle Horace.

Uncle Horace was properly angry at Dr. Wolf. "Thank God and Mortimer that you were saved from his clutches," he said with feeling, after Herbert had told him the whole story of the mongrel's meanness.

That night, Herbert slept peacefully with no bad dreams, as the rocket zoomed through space, eating up thousands and thousands of miles.

The next day, Herbert tried to fill in all he had missed telling Uncle Horace the day before. His uncle complimented him for his success in introducing baseball and scouting to young dogs from the best families on the planet.

"They will no doubt teach others," said Uncle Horace.

"By the time I revisit the dog planet there will probably be dozens of Dog Scout troops," said Herbert. "And Prince won't let them forget that I was the founder of the Dog Scouts."

"Herbert," said Uncle Horace, "I regret to inform you that, for the time being, your chances of revisiting the dog planet are dim."

"How come?" Herbert wanted to know, for it seemed to him that after two successful flights had been made to the dog planet, it might not be long before a regular schedule of flights might be established.

"The night before my take-off," said Uncle

Horace, "the building which served Dr. Gebhart both as laboratory and dwelling burned to the ground. Fortunately, the tower containing the rocket was saved. Dr. Gebhart burned his hands quite badly fighting the fire. It was providential that the rocket was already fueled and the automatic pilot set both for the flight to the planet you were on and the rocket's return to Earth. Otherwise, I would not have been able to come after you for a long time — if ever — for all of Dr. Gebhart's charts and formulas were destroyed. Dr. Gebhart is in hopes of rediscovering the intricate formula of the highly concentrated fuel and making new charts, but it will take time. Of course, I am having a new laboratory built for him."

"Poor Dr. Gebhart!" said Herbert with sympathy. He was disappointed that it might be a long time before he would be seeing his good friend Prince, again, but he cheered up when he thought of the welcome he would receive when he landed on earth, the first person who had visited the dog planet.

"Bet I'm the first one who has ever gone to the dogs and come back," he said jokingly to Uncle Horace. "Won't my parents be surprised when they learn where I really spent my summer vacation. And will I have a lot to tell Pete, Donny, and Chuck. I'll call a special meeting of the *Up in the Air Club* and read my diary to the fellers. Will their eyes bug out! Guess I'll have to get used to being famous," he said. "Naturally, Dr. Gebhart will be famous, too," he added generously.

"Herbert," said Uncle Horace, "I am going to ask you to do something which will be hard for you. I am asking you to talk to nobody except the Gebharts and myself about where you've been or what you've seen. It must, for the time being, remain a secret between us."

Herbert was indignant. "But I've always written a composition the first week of school about where I've spent my summer vacation. And the one I'd write now would be a humdinger."

"With no tangible proof that you have visited a planet where dogs walk like men and have as much — if not more — intelligence, who do you think would believe you? I would not even risk their believing me. Our visits to the dog planet would be called a hoax, and Dr. Gebhart would receive most unpleasant publicity."

"But I have my diary. I can quote from that."

"People would call it science fiction, the product of your fertile imagination," said Uncle Horace.

"That would be the same as calling me a liar," cried Herbert.

"There are often truths so strange that they require a great deal of proof before people will believe them," said Uncle Horace.

"I should have taken pictures," said Herbert. "I could kick myself for not taking pictures. I don't even have a photograph of Prince, and he's the nicest dog — except Mortimer — I've ever known. But I'll remember Prince. He's one dog I'll never forget."

For a few hours, Herbert was unable to get over his disappointment at not being able to tell the world about his adventures. He had cherished the hope of being met with a band and, later on, maybe going to New York City and being the hero in a parade. With Dr. Gebhart sharing the glory, of course. "For I wouldn't expect to hog it all," thought Herbert. But this was not to be. "Oh, well, I'll just have to postpone being famous," he decided, and cheered up.

Herbert and his uncle found it exciting to see the great ball of Earth appear. It was thrilling to watch oceans, mountains, rivers, and cities come into view. Then there were minutes of suspense when the rocket slowed its speed and neared the earth. Herbert, as well as Uncle Horace, gave a sigh of relief when the rocket ejected its legs and came down in full sunlight near the burned place where Dr. Gebhart's combination laboratory and dwelling had stood. A tent was there instead.

"It's a smart rocket that knows its way home," said Herbert as he and his uncle unbuckled the straps which had held them in their contour seats. "Say," he said, "if the Russians should happen to land a man on the dog planet before we Americans get there again, they'll sure be surprised to see a big statue of me right in the middle of City Hall Square."

"They will indeed," said Uncle Horace.

Author's Note

Hazel Wilson was born in Portland and received her B.A. and M.A. from Bates College in Maine. For ten years, she did library work in Maine, Massachusetts, Missouri, Colorado, and Paris. For many years now she has made her home in Washington, D.C. where she keeps busy writing, lecturing, and teaching a course at George Washington University in children's literature. She reviews children's books for the *Washington Star*.

A NOTE ON THE TYPE

The text of this book has been set on the Linotype in Baskerville, a recutting of a type face originally designed by John Baskerville (1706-1775). Baskerville, who was a writing master in Birmingham, England, began experimenting about 1750 with type design and punch cutting. His first book, set throughout in his new types, was a Virgil in royal quarto, published in 1757. His types, which are distinctive and elegant in design, were a forerunner of what we know today as the "modern" group of type faces.